Paris War Days

Charles Inman Barnard

Contents

PARIS WAR DAYS

BY

Charles Inman Barnard

TO

Ogden Mills Reid

EDITOR OF THE NEW YORK TRIBUNE

THIS DIARY IS DEDICATED

IN AFFECTIONATE MEMORY OF

HIS FATHER, THE LATE

Whitelaw Reid

PREFACE

This is not a story of the world-wide war. These notes, jotted down at odd moments in a diary, are published with the idea of recording, day by day, the aspect, temper, mood, and humor of Paris, when the entire manhood of France responds with profound spontaneous patriotism to the call of mobilization in defense of national existence. France is herself again. Her capital, during this supreme trial, is a new Paris, the like of which, after the present crisis is over, will probably not be seen again by any one now living.

As a youth in the spring of 1871, I witnessed Paris, partly in ruins, emerging from the scourges of German invasion and of the Commune. As a correspondent of the **New York Herald**, under the personal direction of my chief, Mr. James Gordon Bennett--for whom I retain a deep-rooted friendship and admiration for his sterling, rugged qualities of a true American and a masterly journalist--it was my good fortune, during fourteen years, to share the joys and charms of Parisian life. I was in Paris during the throes of the Dreyfus affair when, at the call of the late Whitelaw Reid, I began my duties as resident correspondent of the **New York Tribune**. I saw Paris suffer the winter floods of 1910. Whether in storm or in sunshine, I have always found myself among friends in this vivacious center of humanity, intelligence, art, science, and sentiment, where our countrymen, and above all our country-women, realize that they have a second home. With a finger on the pulse, as it were, of Paris, I have sought to register the throbs and feelings of Parisians and Americans during these war days. I acknowledge deep indebtedness to the European edition of the **New York Herald**, and to the Continental edition of the **Daily Mail**, from whose columns useful data and information have been freely drawn.

C. I. B.

Paris, October, 1914.

PARIS WAR DAYS

Saturday, August 1, 1914

This war comes like the traditional "Bolt from the Blue!" I had made arrangements to retire from active journalism and relinquish the duties of Paris correspondent of the ***New York Tribune***, which I had fulfilled for sixteen consecutive years. In reply to a request from Mr. Ogden Reid, I had expressed willingness to remain at my post in Paris until the early autumn, inasmuch as "a quiet summer was expected." Spring was a busy time for newspaper men. There had been the sensational assassination of Gaston Calmette, editor of the ***Figaro***, by Mme. Caillaux, wife of the cabinet minister. Then there was the "caving-in" of the streets of Paris, owing to the effect of storms on the thin surface left by the underground tunnelling for the electric tramways, and for the new metropolitan "tubes." The big prize fight between Jack Johnson and Frank Moran for the heavy-weight championship of the world followed. Next came the trial of Mme. Caillaux and her acquittal. Then followed the newspaper campaign of the brothers, MM. Paul and Guy de Cassagnac, against German newspaper correspondents in Paris. The Cassagnacs demanded that certain German correspondents should quit French territory within twenty-four hours. As several German correspondents were members of the "Association of the Foreign Press," of which I happen to be president, I was able to smooth matters over a little. Although my personal sympathies were strongly with the Cassagnacs, who are editors of ***L'Autorite***, especially in their condemnation of the severity of the German Government in regard to "Hansi," the Alsatian caricaturist and author of ***Mon Village***, I managed with the help of some of my Russian, Italian, English, and Spanish colleagues to avoid needless duels and quarrels between French and German journalists. Finally, the day of the "Grand Prix de Paris" brought the news of the murder at Sarajevo of the heir to the Austro-Hungarian throne. My friend, Mr. Edward Schuler, was despatched by the Associated Press to Vienna, and when he returned, I readily saw, from the state of feeling that he described as existing in Vienna, that war between Austria and Servia was inevitable, and that unless some supreme effort should be made for peace by Emperor William, a general European war must follow.

Wednesday, July 29, the day after Austria's declaration of war against Servia, I lunched at the Hotel Ritz with Mrs. Marshall Field and her nephew, Mr. Spencer Eddy. Mrs. Field was about to leave Paris for Aix-les-Bains. We talked about the probability of Russia being forced to make war with Germany. I warned Mrs. Field of the risk she would run in going to Aix-les-Bains, and in the event of mobilization, of being deprived of her motor-car and of all means of getting away. At that time no one seemed to think that war really would break out. Mrs. Field finally gave up her plan of going to Aix-les-Bains and went to London. The following evening Maitre Charles Philippe of the Paris Bar and M. Max-Lyon, a French railroad engineer who had built many of the Turkish and Servian railroads, dined with me. They both felt that nothing could now avert war between France and Germany.

Yesterday (July 31) a sort of war fever permeated the air. A cabinet minister assured me that at whatever capital there was the slightest hope of engaging in negotiations and compromise, at that very point the "mailed fist" diplomacy of the Kaiser William dealt an unexpected blow. There seems no longer any hope for peace, because it is evident that the Military Pretorian Guard, advisers to the German and Austrian emperors, are in the ascendency, and they want war. "Very well, they will have it!" remarked the veteran French statesman, M. Georges Clemenceau.

After dinner last evening I happened to be near the Cafe du Croissant near the Bourse and in the heart of the newspaper quarter of Paris. Suddenly an excited crowd collected. "Jaures has been assassinated!" shouted a waiter. The French deputy and anti-war agitator was sitting with his friends at a table near an open window in the cafe. A young Frenchman named Raoul Villain, son of a clerk of the Civil Court of Rheims, pushed a revolver through the window and shot Jaures through the head. He died a few moments later. The murder of the socialist leader would in ordinary times have so aroused party hatred that almost civil war would have broken out in Paris. But to-night, under the tremendous patriotic pressure of the German emperor's impending onslaught upon France, the whole nation is united as one man. As M. Arthur Meyer, editor of the *Gaulois*, remarked: "France is now herself again! Not since a hundred years has the world seen '*France Debout!*'"

At four o'clock this afternoon I was standing on the Place de la Bourse when the mobilization notices were posted. Paris seemed electrified. All cabs were immediately taken. I walked to the Place de l'Opera and Rue de la Paix to note the effect of the mobilization call upon the people. Crowds of young men, with French flags, promenaded the streets, shouting "Vive La France!" Bevies of young sewing-girls, *midinettes*, collected at the open windows and on the balconies of the Rue de la Paix, cheering, waving their handkerchiefs at the youthful patriots, and throwing down upon them handfuls of flowers and garlands that had decked the fronts of the shops. The crowd was not particularly noisy or boisterous. No cries of "On to Berlin!" or "Down with the Germans!" were heard. The shouts that predominated were simply: "Vive La France!" "Vive l'Armee!" and "Vive l'Angleterre!" One or two British flags were also borne along beside the French tricolor.

I cabled the following message to Mr. Ogden Reid, editor of the *New York Tribune*:

> ribune, New York, Private for Mr. Reid. Suggest
> supreme importance event hostilities of Brussels as center
> of all war news. Also that Harry Lawson, *Daily Telegraph*,
> London, is open any propositions coming from you
> concerning *Tribune* sharing war news service with his
> paper. According best military information be useless
> expense sending special men to front with French owing
> absolute rigid censorship.

BARNARD.

I based this suggestion about the supreme importance of Brussels because it has for years been an open secret among military men that the only hope of the famous *attaque brusquee* of the German armies being successful would be by violating Belgian neutrality and swarming in like wasps near Liege and Namur, and surprising the French mobilization by sweeping by the lines of forts constructed by the foremost military engineer in Europe, the late Belgian general, De Brialmont.

I subsequently received a cable message from the editor of the **Tribune** expressing the wish to count upon my services during the present crisis. To this I promptly agreed.

Sunday, August 2.

This is the first day of mobilization. I looked out of the dining-room window of my apartment at Number 8 Rue Theodule-Ribot at four this morning. Already the streets resounded with the buzz, whirl, and horns of motor-cars speeding along the Boulevard de Courcelles, and the excited conversation of men and women gathered in groups on the sidewalks. It was warm, rather cloudy weather. Thermometer, 20 degrees centigrade, with light, southwesterly breezes. My servant, Felicien, summoned by the mobilization notices calling out the reservists, was getting ready to join his regiment, the Thirty-second Dragoons. His young wife and child had arrived the day before from Brittany. My housekeeper, Sophie, who was born in Baden-Baden and came to Paris with her mother when a girl of eight, is in great anxiety lest she be expelled, owing to her German nationality.

I walked to the chancellery of the American Embassy, Number 5 Rue de Chaillot, where fifty stranded Americans were vainly asking the clerks how they could get away from Paris and how they could have their letters of credit cashed. Three stray Americans drove up in a one-horse cab. I took the cab, after it had been discharged, and went to the Ministry of Foreign Affairs, where I expected to find our Ambassador, Mr. Myron T. Herrick. M. Viviani, the President of the Council of Ministers and Minister of Foreign Affairs, was there awaiting the arrival of Baron de Schoen, the German Ambassador, who had made an appointment for eleven o'clock. It was now half-past eleven, and his German excellency had not yet come.

I watched the arrival of the St. Cyr cadets at the Gare d'Orsay station on their way to the Gare de l'Est. These young French "West Pointers" are sturdy, active, wiry little chaps, brimful of pluck, intelligence, and determination. They carried their bags and boxes in their hands, and their overcoats were neatly folded *bandeliere* fashion from the right shoulder to the left hip. Then came a couple of hundred requisitioned horses led by cavalrymen. Driving by the Invalides, I noticed about five hundred requisitioned automobiles. I was very much impressed by the earnest, grave determination of the reservists, who were silently rejoining their posts. Some of them were accompanied by wives, sisters, or sweethearts, who concealed their tears with forced smiles. Now and then groups of young men escorted the reservists, singing the "Marseillaise" and waving French, British, and Russian flags. At the Place de la Concorde, near the statue of "Strasbourg," was a procession of Italians, who had offered their military services to the Minister of War in spite of Italy's obligation to the Triple Alliance.

Later, at the American Embassy, Number 5 Rue Francois Premier, I found Ambassador Herrick arranging for a sort of relief committee of Americans to aid and regulate the situation of our stranded countrymen and women here. There are about three thousand who want to get home, but who are unable to obtain money on their letters of credit; if they have money, they are unable to find trains, or passenger space on westward bound liners. Mr. Herrick showed me a cablegram from the State Department at Washington instructing him to remain at his post until his successor, Mr. Sharp, can reach Paris; also to inform Mr. Thomas Nelson Page, American Ambassador at Rome, to cancel his leave of absence and stop in Rome, even if "Italy had decided to remain neutral." As soon as the German and Austro-Hungarian ambassadors quit the capital, Mr. Herrick will be placed in charge of all the German and Austro-Hungarian subjects left behind here. I met also M. J. J. Jusserand, French Ambassador at Washington, who intends sailing Tuesday for New York. M. Jusserand informed me that official news had reached the Paris Ministry of the Interior of Germany's violation of the territory of Luxemburg, the independence of which had been guaranteed by the Powers, including of course Prussia, by the Treaty of London in 1867. M. Jusserand was very indignant at this reckless breach of international law.

At the suggestion of Mr. Herrick, a committee of Americans was chosen to co-operate with him in giving such information and advice to Americans in Paris as the efforts of the committee to ascertain facts and conditions may justify. The committee think there is no cause for alarm on the part of those who remain in the city for the present; and that Americans will be able to leave at some later date, if any desire to do so.

The committee will endeavor to learn what can be done in securing money on letters of credit or travelers' cheques, or in getting means of transportation to such places as they may desire to go.

The committee includes Messrs. Laurence B. Benet, W.S. Dalliba, Charles Carroll, Frederick Coudert, James Deering, Chauncey M. Depew, E.H. Gary, H. Herman Harjes, William Jay, F.B. Kellog, Percy Peixotto, and Henry S. Priest. The chairman is Judge E.H. Gary.

Mr. Herrick asked me to convey a private message to one of his friends, but as the telephone service was interrupted, Mr. Laurence Norton, the Ambassador's secretary, loaned me his motor-car for the purpose. On the Cour La Reine a procession of young men escorting reservists and bearing a French flag appeared. I naturally raised my hat to salute the colors. The crowd, noticing the red, white, and blue cockades on the hats of the chauffeur and the footman, mistook me for the American Ambassador or for a cabinet minister, and burst into frantic cheers.

In the German quarter, near the Rue d'Hauteville, a couple of German socialists who were so imprudent as to shout "***A bas l'armee!***" were surrounded by angry Frenchmen, and despite an attempt of the police to protect them, were very roughly handled. A German shoemaker who attempted to charge exaggerated prices for boots had his windows smashed and his stock looted by an infuriated crowd.

The news that the German shops were being attacked soon spread, and youths gathered in bands, going from one shop to the other and wrecking them in the course of a few moments. Further riots occurred near the Gare de l'Est, a district which is inhabited by a large number of Germans. A great deal of damage was done.

Measures were taken at once by the authorities, and several cavalry detachments were called to the aid of the police. The youths were quite docile on the whole, a word from a policeman being sufficient to turn them away.

The cavalry, too, only made a few charges at a sharp trot and were received with hearty cheers. Policemen and municipal guards were, however, stationed before shops known to be owned by Germans.

In spite of this rioting, responsible Parisians may be said to have remained as calm as they have been all through this critical time. Among those taking part in wrecking shops were few people older than seventeen or eighteen.

Already the familiar aspect of the Parisian street crowd has changed. It is now composed almost exclusively of men either too young or too old for military service and of women and children. Most of the younger generation have already left to join corps on the front or elsewhere in France. It is impossible to spend more than a few minutes in the streets without witnessing scenes which speak of war.

There are long processions of vehicles of all sorts, market carts, two-wheeled lorries, furniture vans, all of them stocked with rifles for the reserves and all of them led or driven by soldiers.

Not a motor-omnibus is to be seen. The taxi-cabs and cabs are scarce. Tramway-cars are running, although on some lines the service is reduced considerably. In spite of the disorganization of traffic, the majority of Parisians go about their business quietly.

There is deep confidence in the national cause. "We did not want this war, but as Germany has begun we will fight, and Germany will find that the heart of France is in a war for freedom," is an expression heard on all sides.

Everywhere there are touching scenes. In the early hours of the morning a *chasseur* covered with dust, who had come to bid farewell to his family, was seen riding through the city. As he rode down the street, an old woman stopped him and said: "Do your best! They killed my husband in '70." The young soldier stooped from his saddle and silently gripped the old woman's hand.

Monday, August 3.

This is the second day of mobilization. A warm, cloudy day with occasional showers. Thermometer, 20 degrees centigrade.

At six this morning Felicien, with a brown paper parcel containing a day's rations consisting of cold roast beef, sandwiches, hard-boiled eggs, bread, butter, and potato salad, walked off to the Gare St. Lazare, which is his point of rendezvous indicated by the mobilization paper. His young wife wept as if broken-hearted. Felicien, like all the reservists, restrained his emotions. I shook him warmly by the hand and said that I would surely see him again here within six months, and that he would come home a victor. "Don't be afraid of that, sir!" was his reply, and away he went.

I watched the looting of the Maggi milk shops near the Place des Ternes. The marauders were youths from fifteen to eighteen years old, and seemed to have no idea of the crimes they were committing. The Maggi is no longer a German enterprise, and the stupid acts of these young ruffians can only have the effect of depriving French mothers and infants of much-needed milk. I bought a bicycle to-day at Peugeot's in the Avenue of the Grande Armee, because it is hopeless to get cabs or motor-cabs. While there, the shop was requisitioned by an officer, who took away with him three hundred bicycles for the army.

The aspect of the main thoroughfares in the Opera quarter, the center of English and American tourist traffic, was depressing in the extreme this afternoon. All the shipping offices in the Rue Scribe closed in the morning. The Rue de la Paix is never very brilliant in August, but now it is an abode of desolation. Nine tenths of the shops have their shutters up and the jewelers who keep open have withdrawn all their stock from the windows.

Many of the closed shops on the boulevards and elsewhere bear placards designed to protect them from the possible attentions of the mob. On these placards are such texts as "Maison Francaise" or even "Maison ultrafrancaise."

On the Cafe de la Paix is the following announcement, in several places: "The proprietor, Andre Millon, who is mayor of Evecquemont (Seine-et-Oise), has been called out for service in the army and left this morning." Similar messages, written in chalk, are to be seen on hundreds of shutters.

Steps have been taken at the American Embassy to supply credentials, in the form of "a paper of nationality," to citizens of the United States, which will make it possible for them to register as such with the police, as required by the French Government.

The proposed American Ambulance has been organized under the official patronage of Ambassador Herrick, and the auspices of the American Hospital of Paris.

Beginning to-day, all cafes and restaurants will be closed at eight in the evening. They were left open till nine yesterday as an exceptional measure, owing to the fact that there was not time to distribute the order for early closing by eight o'clock.

The aspect of the boulevards last night was the completest possible contrast to what was seen on Sunday night. The city was under martial law, and the police showed very plainly that they did not intend to be trifled with.

Instead of shouting crowds and stone-throwing by excited youths and women, one saw only a few citizens walking slowly along. One group of policemen took shelter from the intermittent showers under the marquise of the Vaudeville Theater, and other detachments were in readiness at corners all along the line of the boulevards, which were dotted with isolated policemen.

No one was allowed to loiter. To wait five minutes outside a house was to court investigation and possibly arrest. There was no sound except that of footfalls and a low murmur of conversation. It was the first night of war's stern government.

Germany officially declared war upon France at five forty-five this evening. The notification was made by Baron von Schoen, the German Ambassador to France, when he called at the Ministry of Foreign Affairs to ask for his passports.

Baron von Schoen declared that his Government had instructed him to inform the Government of the Republic that French aviators had flown over Belgium and that other French aviators had flown over Germany and dropped bombs as far as Nuremberg. He added that this constituted an act of aggression and violation of German territory.

M. Viviani listened in silence to Baron von Schoen's statement, and when the German Ambassador had finished, replied that it was absolutely false that French aviators had flown over Belgium and Germany and had dropped bombs.

Immediately after this interview, M. Viviani telegraphed to M. Jules Cambon, French Ambassador in Berlin, instructing him to immediately ask for his passports and to make a report on France's protest against the violation of the neutrality of Luxemburg and the ultimatum sent to Belgium. M. Cambon will leave Berlin tomorrow.

Since acts of war were committed by German troops two days ago, the delay in the recall of the German Ambassador had appeared inexplicable to the great majority of French people, to whom Baron von Schoen appeared to be decidedly outstopping his welcome.

The Ambassador himself seemed conscious of this feeling, for not only did he take care to proceed to the Quai d'Orsay in as inconspicuous a manner as possible, but he also applied to the authorities to detail a policeman to accompany him in his automobile.

Baron von Schoen's departure from Paris was a solemn affair. He left the Embassy last, after a vast collection of luggage had gone off in motor-wagons and other vehicles. A few minutes before ten o'clock, wearing a soft felt hat and black frock coat adorned with the rosette of the Legion of Honor and carrying a rainproof coat over his arm, he left in a powerful automobile, which, by way of the Invalides, the Trocadero, and the Boulevard Flandrin, conveyed him to the station.

The station employes and the police on duty at the station formed a silent cordon, through which the departing Ambassador passed with downcast eyes.

Not a word was spoken as the baron stood for a few minutes on the platform.

Then the stationmaster said quietly: "*En voiture*," there was a shrill whistle, and the train, composed of five coaches and three goods trucks, glided slowly out of the station.

Tuesday, August 4.

We are now in the third day of mobilization. Weather slightly cooler, 17 degrees centigrade, with moderate southwest wind.

At seven this morning I went with Sophie to the registration office for Germans, Alsatians, and Austro-Hungarians, Number 213 Place Boulevard Periere. A crowd of some five hundred persons--men, women, and children--were waiting at the doors of the public schoolroom now used as the *Siege du District* for the seventeenth arrondissement. Although a German by birth, Sophie is French at heart. She came to Paris when only eight years old and has remained here ever since--she is now sixty-one--and has been thirty-two years with me as housekeeper and cook. All her German relatives are dead. Hers is a hard case, for if expelled from France, she would have to become practically a stranger in a strange land. Fortunately she has all her papers in order, and can show that she has nine nephews actually in the French army. I made a statement in writing for her to this effect, which she took to the registration office, but she had to wait, standing without shelter from eight in the morning to six o'clock at night. After carefully scrutinizing her papers, the officials told her that her papers must go for inspection to the Prefecture of Police, and that she must come back for them to-morrow. She had with her photographs of three of her nephews in military uniforms. One of these nephews had received a decoration during the Morocco campaign for saving his captain's life during an engagement.

I managed to see the Commissary of Police of the quarter and spoke to him about Sophie, explaining her case and saying that as she was such a splendid cook it would be a great pity if Paris should lose her services. The commissary smiled and said: "It will be all right. Sophie will be allowed to remain in Paris!" I profited by the occasion to obtain a ***permis de sejour***, or residence permit, for myself. The commissary, after noting on paper my personal description and measuring my height, handed me the precious document authorizing me to reside in the "entrenched camp of Paris." These papers must be kept on one's person, ready to be shown whenever called for. Outside of the office about three hundred foreigners, including Emile Wauters, the Belgian painter, and several well-known Americans and English, were waiting their turn to get into the office. I congratulated myself on having a journalist's ***coupe-file*** card that had enabled me to get in before the others, some of whom stood waiting for six hours before their turn came. This is an instance of stupid French bureaucracy or red-tapism. It would have been very easy to have distributed numbers to those waiting, and the applicants would then have been able, by calculating the time, to go about their business and return when necessary. Another instance of this fatal red-tapism of French officialdom came in the shape of a summons from the fiscal office of Vernon, where I have a little country place on the Seine, to pay the sum of two francs, which is the annual tax for a float I had there for boating purposes. This trivial paper, coming in amidst the whirlpool of mobilization, displays the mentality of the provincial officials.

After doing some writing, I went on my new bicycle to the chancellery of the United States Embassy and saw a crowd of about seventy Americans on the sidewalk awaiting their turn to obtain identification papers. I met here Mr. Bernard J. Schoninger, former president of the American Chamber of Commerce in Paris. The news of the outbreak of war found him at Luchon in the Pyrenees. All train service being monopolized for the troops, he came in his automobile to Paris, a distance of about a thousand kilometers. All went smoothly until he reached Tours, when he was held up at every five kilometers by guards who demanded his papers. Chains or ropes were often stretched across the roads. Mr. Schoninger showed the guards his visiting card, explained who he was, and said that he was going to Paris on purpose to get his papers. The authorities were very civil, as they usually are to all Americans who approach them politely, and allowed him to motor to Neuilly, just outside the fortifications of Paris.

I proceeded on my wheel to the Embassy, where I found our Ambassador very busy with the American Relief Committee and with the American Ambulance people.

Several Americans at the Embassy were making impractical requests, as for instance that the American Ambassador demand that the French Government accept the passports or identification papers issued by the American Embassy here in lieu of ***permis de sejour***. If the French Government accorded this favor to the United States, all the other neutral nations would require the same privilege, and thus in time of war, with fighting going on only a little over two hundred kilometers from Paris, the French Government would lose direct control of permission for foreigners to remain in the capital.

It is estimated that there are over forty thousand Americans at present stranded in Europe, seventy-five hundred of them being in Paris. Of these fifteen hundred are without present means.

The Embassy is literally besieged by hundreds of these unfortunate travelers. There were so many of them, and their demands were so urgent, that the Military Attache, Major Spencer Cosby, had to utilize the services of eight American army officers on leave to form a sort of guard to control their compatriots. These officers were Major Morton John Henry, Captain Frank Parker, Captain Francis H. Pope, Lieutenants B.B. Summerwell, F.W. Honeycutt, Joseph B. Treat, J.H. Jouett, and H.F. Loomis. The last four are young graduates of West Point, the others being on the active list of the United States army.

Ambassador Herrick set his face against any favoritism in receiving the applicants, and some very prominent citizens had to stand in line for hours before they could be admitted. Mr. Oscar Underwood, son of Senator-elect Underwood, is organizing means to alleviate the distress among his countrymen and countrywomen in Paris. He has also asked the Ministry of Foreign Affairs to extend the time allowed for Americans to obtain formal permission to remain in France, and his request will no doubt be granted.

Doctor Watson, rector of the American Church of the Holy Trinity, in the Avenue de l'Alma, has offered that building as temporary sleeping quarters for Americans who are unable to obtain shelter elsewhere, and is arranging to hold some trained nurses at the disposal of the feeble and sick.

War is a wonderful leveler, but there could hardly be a greater piece of irony perpetrated by Fate than compelling well-to-do Americans, who have no share in the quarrel on hand, to sleep in a church in France like destitutes before any of the French themselves are called upon to undergo such an experience.

At the Chamber of Deputies I witnessed a historic scene never to be forgotten. Some of the deputies were reservists and had come in their uniforms, but the rules prevented them from taking their seats in military attire. In the Diplomatic Tribune sat Sir Francis Bertie, the British Ambassador, side by side with M. Alexander Iswolsky, the Russian Ambassador. The Chamber filled in complete silence. The whole House, from royalists to socialists, listened, standing, to a glowing tribute by M. Paul Deschanel, president of the Chamber, to M. Jaures, over whose coffin, he said, the whole of France was united. "There are no more adversaries," exclaimed M. Deschanel, with a voice trembling with emotion, "there are only Frenchmen." The whole house as one man raised a resounding shout of "Vive la France!"

When M. Deschanel concluded, there was a pause during the absence of M. Viviani. The Premier entered, pale but confident, amid a hurricane of cheers and read amid a silence broken only by frenzied shouts of "Vive la France!" a speech detailing the whole course of the diplomatic negotiations, in which he placed upon Germany crushing responsibility for the catastrophe which has overtaken Europe.

The Chamber, before rising, adopted unanimously without discussion a whole series of bills making provision for national defense and the maintenance of order in France.

M. Viviani's speech was interrupted by terrific cheering when he referred to the attitude adopted by the British and Belgian governments. All rose to face the diplomatic tribune, cheering again and again.

M. Viviani's last phrase, "We are without reproach. We shall be without fear," swept the whole Chamber off its feet.

The vast hemicycle was a compact mass of cheering deputies, all waving aloft in their hands papers and handkerchiefs. From the tribunes of the public gallery shout after shout went up. At the foot of the presidential platform the gray-haired usher, with his 1870 war medals on his breasts, was seated, overcome with emotion, the tears coursing down his cheeks.

Paris is back in the days of the curfew, and at eight o'clock, by order of the Military Governor of Paris, it is "lights out" on the boulevards, all the cafes close their doors, the underground railway ceases running, and policemen and sentinels challenge any one going home late, lest he should be a German spy. Paris is no longer "*la ville lumiere*"-- it is a sad and gloomy city, where men and women go about with solemn, anxious faces, and every conversation seems to begin and end with the dreadful word "War!"

There is no more rioting in the streets. The bands of young blackguards who went about pillaging the shops of inoffensive citizens have been cleared from the streets, and demonstrations of every kind are strictly forbidden. So far is this carried that a cab was stopped at the Madeleine, and a policeman ordered the cab driver to take the little French flag out of the horse's collar.

In the evening the city is wrapped in a silence which makes it difficult to realize that one is in the capital of a great commercial center. The smallest of provincial villages would seem lively compared with the boulevards last night. But for large numbers of policemen and occasional military patrols, the streets were practically deserted.

There is, however, nothing for the police to do, for the sternly worded announcement that disturbers of the peace would be court-martialed had the instant effect of putting a stop to any noisy demonstrations, let alone any attempts at pillage. Policemen can be seen sitting about on doorsteps or leaning against trees.

Parisians are already going through a small revival of what they did during the siege of 1871. They are lining up at regular hours outside provision shops and waiting their turn to be served. Many large groceries are open only from nine to eleven in the morning and from three to five in the afternoon, not because there is any scarcity of food, but on account of lack of assistants, all their young men being at the front or on their way there.

Great activity is already being shown in preparing to receive wounded soldiers from the front, and all the ambulance and nursing societies are working hand in hand.

The women of Paris are being enrolled in special schools where they will be taught the art of nursing, and thousands of young women and girls in the provinces have promised to help their country by making uniforms and bandages. Others will look after the children of widowers who have gone to the front, and in various other ways the women of France are justifying their reputation for cheerful self-abnegation.

The Medical Board of the American Hospital held another meeting at the hospital in Neuilly, to consider further the organization of the hospital for wounded soldiers, with an ambulance service, which it is proposed to offer as an American contribution to France in her hour of trouble.

Just how extensive this medical service will be depends upon the amount of money that will be obtained from Americans. The enterprise was given its first impulse at a meeting of the Board of Governors and the Medical Board of the American Hospital held on Monday at the request of Ambassador Herrick.

It is intended to establish at first a hospital of one hundred or two hundred beds, fully equipped to care for wounded French soldiers. Several places are under consideration, but at present no information of a definite character can be given on this subject. Later, if Americans are sufficiently generous in their contributions, it is proposed to obtain from the French Government the use of the Lycee Pasteur in Neuilly, not far from the American Hospital. In this building a thousand beds could be placed, and it is hoped that funds will be available to undertake this larger ambulance service.

Meanwhile the American Hospital at Neuilly is not to be affected in any way by this emergency undertaking, but it will continue its work for Americans in need of medical attention. The special hospital for soldiers is to be an American offering under the auspices of the American Hospital and under the direction of the Medical Board of that institution.

The Medical Board of the American Hospital consists of Doctor Robert Turner, chairman; Doctor Magnier, who is well known as the founder of the hospital; Doctor Debuchet, Doctor Gros, Doctor Koenig and Doctor Whitman.

Mrs. Herrick, Mrs. Potter Palmer, Mrs. Carolan, and other prominent American women have applied for service with the Red Cross.

Wednesday, August 5.
Fourth day of mobilization. Cloudy weather with southwesterly wind, temperature at five P.M. 21 degrees centigrade.

Looking out of the window this morning I noticed British flags waving beside French flags on several balconies and shops. England's declaration of war against Germany arouses tremendous enthusiasm. The heroic defense made by the Belgians against three German army corps advancing on the almost impregnable fortress of Liege--a second Port Arthur--is a magnificent encouragement for the French. At some of the houses in Paris one now sees occasionally assembled the flags of France, Russia, Great Britain, Belgium, and Servia.

Paris is beginning to settle down more or less to the abnormal state of things prevailing in the city since the departure of the reservists. Those who remain behind are showing an admirable spirit. Nowhere are complaints voiced in regard to the complete disorganization of the public services. M. Hennion, chief of police, has devised an excellent means of clearing the streets of dangerous individuals. He has arranged for half a dozen auto-busses containing a dozen policemen to circulate in the different quarters at night. The auto-busses stop now and then, and the police make a silent search for marauders. Any one found with a revolver or a knife is arrested, put in handcuffs, and placed in the auto-bus and carried to the police station.

Sophie at last got her ***permis de sejour*** this evening. The expelled Germans will be sent to a remote station near the Spanish frontier. The undesirable Austro-Hungarians will be relegated to Brittany, where perhaps they may be utilized in harvesting the wheat crop. Germans in the domestic service of French citizens are allowed to remain in Paris.

The French Institute is participating in the campaign reservist mobilization. M. Etienne Lamy, Perpetual Secretary of the French Academy, is a major in the territorial army and is about to take the field. M. Pierre Loti, who is a captain in the navy, will be provided with a suitable command. M. Marcel Prevost, graduate of the Polytechnic School, is a major of artillery, and will command a battery in one of the forts near Paris.

Among American ladies added to the list of those who have volunteered for service with the Red Cross are Mrs. Gary, Mrs. E. Tuck, Mrs. Hickox, Mrs. George Munroe, Mrs. Smith, Mrs. Bell, Mrs. French, Mrs. G. Gray, Mrs. Gurnee, Mrs. Burden, Mrs. Harjes, Mrs. Bennett, Mrs. Dalliba, Mrs. Burnell, Mrs. Farwell, Mrs. Blumenthal, Mrs. Moore, Mrs. Walter Gay, Mrs. Tiffany, Mrs. Allan, Miss Gillett, and

Miss Gurnee.

A number of American and English-speaking physicians and surgeons respond-ed to the appeal made by Doctor J.M. Gershberg, of New York, visiting physician to the Hopital Broca, and attended a meeting held at Professor Pozzi's dispensary to form an organization offering their medical and surgical services to the French Government and the Red Cross Society.

Doctor Gershberg explained that the plan is to form three bodies: a body of English-speaking physicians and surgeons, a body of English-speaking nurses, and a body of English-speaking attendants. The proprietor of the Hotel Chatham, a re-serve officer in the artillery, and M. C. Michaut, ex-reserve officer of artillery, have decided to place the establishment at the disposal of the Red Cross Society for the reception of wounded soldiers.

Americans arriving in Paris from Germany and Switzerland continue to bring stories of hardships inflicted on them by the sudden outbreak of war. Mr. T.C. Es-tee, of New York, who reached Paris with his family, reported that he left behind at Zurich two hundred Americans who apparently had no means of getting away.

He and his family were lucky enough to catch the last train conveying troops westward. They traveled for two days without food or water, one of the ladies faint-ing from exhaustion, and after the train reached its destination they had to walk several miles across the frontier, where they were taken on board a French troop train. They lost all their baggage.

Eight other Americans reported a similar experience. They had a tramp of ten miles into France, and one of their number, a lady partly paralyzed, had to be car-ried. They could procure no food until they reached France. Finally they obtained a motor-car which brought them to Paris. This memorable journey began at Dres-den.

Thursday, August 6.

Fifth day of mobilization. Cloudy in the morning, fair in the afternoon. Ther-mometer at five P.M. 17 degrees centigrade.

Our Ambassador, Mr. Herrick, whom I saw in the afternoon, is delighted with the progress being made with the American Hospital for the French wounded. Mrs.

Herrick is getting on famously with her organization of the woman's committee of the American Ambulance of Paris, which is to be offered to the French Military Government for the aid of wounded soldiers.

Mrs. Herrick was elected president of the committee, Mrs. Potter Palmer vice-president, Mrs. H. Herman Harjes treasurer, and Mrs. Laurence V. Benet secretary. An executive committee was then elected, consisting of Mrs. Laurence V. Benet, Mrs. H. Herman Harjes, Mrs. Potter Palmer, Mrs. Carroll of Carrollton, and Mrs. George Munroe.

Among the women present at the meeting, in addition to those already named, were: Mrs. Elbert H. Gary, Mrs. William Jay, Mrs. A. M. Thackara, Mrs. James Henry Smith, Mrs. J. Burden, Mrs. Dalliba, Mrs. Blumenthal, Mrs. Walter Gay, Mrs. Tuck, Mrs. Charles Barney, Mrs. Whitney Warren, Mrs. Philip Lydig, Mrs. Hickox, Mrs. F. Bell, Mrs. French, Mrs. Frederick Allen, Mrs. Farwell, Miss Edyth Deacon, Mrs. Cameron, Mrs. William Crocker, Mrs. Herman B. Duryea, Mrs. Roche, Miss Hallmark, Mrs. Robert Bliss, Mrs. Crosby, Mrs. Webb, Mrs. Howe, Miss Allen, Mrs. Carolan and Mrs. Marcou.

At the Embassy, I met Colonel William Jay, whom I had known as a boy when he was aide-de-camp to General Meade, then in command of the Army of the Potomac. We talked about the prospects of the war and especially of the Belgians' superb defense at Liege and also discussed the report that a British force had been transported to Havre. I called at the Ministry of War this morning, and Colonel Commandant Duval, chief of the press bureau there, gave me a *laisser-passer* to enter the Ministry three times a day: ten in the morning, three in the afternoon, and at eleven o'clock at night to get the official news communicated by the War Department to the newspapers. It is odd to notice the martial aspect of the door-keepers and ushers at the War Office. Their moustaches have become longer and fiercer, and their replies to most trivial questions are pronounced with an air of impressive mystery. At the War Office, I met M. Louis Barthou, former prime minister, who expressed genuine enthusiasm at the heroic fighting of the Belgians. I afterwards went to the Ministry of Foreign Affairs to see about having my *coupe-file*, or special pass, vised with a *laisser-passer* label. This can only be obtained at the Prefecture of Police upon the special authorization of the Foreign Office. I was told that although a few such permits had been granted, no decision will be taken in the matter before Saturday.

M. Jusserand, French Ambassador at Washington, together with his wife, made a vain attempt a few days ago to reach Havre in time to catch the ***France***, which sailed before her schedule time--a precautionary measure, taken, it is said, to elude German cruisers. M. and Mme. Jusserand consequently failed to catch the liner and returned to Paris.

Much to my surprise, Felicien, my servant, turned up at six P.M., having obtained leave from the reserve squadron of his regiment, the Thirty-second Dragoons at Versailles, to visit his wife in Paris. The active squadrons of his regiment are at Chalons. The married reservists are held back until the others have gone to the front. This system is likely to be an economical one, for all the widows of soldiers killed in the war will have fairly good pensions.

There is probably no more forlorn street in Paris at the present moment than the Rue de la Paix, the headquarters for dressmakers and milliners. Upwards of seventy-five per cent. of the shops are closed, and on both sides the street presents a long, gray expanse--broken only at intervals--of forbidding iron shutters.

It is not here, however, that one must look for the effect of the war on American business, but rather along the Avenue de l'Opera, the Grand Boulevards, and other well-known business streets.

In the Avenue de l'Opera, at the intersection of the Rue Louis-le-Grand, the Paris shop of the Singer Sewing Machine Company is closed, while on the other side Hanan's boot and shoe store is also shut. Just off the avenue, where the Rue des Pyramides cuts in, the establishment where the Colgate and the Chesebrough companies exploit their products likewise presents barred doors. Two conspicuous American establishments remaining open in the Avenue de l'Opera are the Butterick shop and Brentano's.

Mr. Lewis J. Ford, manager of Brentano's, said that they had lost a quarter of their employes and fifty per cent. of their trade by reason of the war, but proposed to keep open just the same.

In the Grand Boulevards the Remington typewriter headquarters are closed, as is the Spalding shop for athletic supplies; but the establishments of the Walkover Shoe Company, both on the Boulevard des Capucines and the Boulevard des Italiens, are open.

In spite of the hardship entailed upon American firms, they are far from complaining. On the contrary, there is a concerted movement among American business men at this time to assist the French in keeping the industrial life of Paris going as normally as possible during the war.

At night Paris is still dark and silent, but in the daytime the city is beginning to adapt itself to the new state of things. Many places from which the men have been called away to serve their country are being filled by women.

Women are becoming tramway conductors, and there is talk of their working the underground railway. Girl clerks are taking places in government and other offices.

The unusual state of things prevailing in Paris is the cause of many picturesque scenes. This morning there was an unwonted sight of a hundred cows being driven by herdsmen of rustic appearance along the Boulevard des Capucines. A little further on, the eye was arrested by a brilliant mass of red and blue on the steps of the Madeleine, where a number of men of the Second Cuirassiers were attending special mass.

The cheerful tone which prevails among the people in the street is very noticeable. All faces are smiling and give the impression of a holiday crowd out enjoying themselves at the national fete, an impression which is reinforced by the gay display of bunting in most of the streets in the center of Paris.

A remarkable sight is the Rue du Croissant in the afternoon, at the time when the evening newspapers are printed. The unusual number of papers sold in the streets has brought thousands of boys, girls, women, and old men from the outlying districts of the city.

There are thousands of them eagerly awaiting the appearance of the ***Presse***, ***Intransigeant***, and other papers. The narrow, picturesque old street is one seething mass of human beings. Hundreds also wait in the Rue Montmartre. As they wait, they pass the time by playing cards or dice.

Many industries are severely affected owing to the absence of men. One of them is the laundry industry, which is unable to deliver washing, owing to the want of vehicles and drivers. In consequence, many Parisians have now adopted the soft collar. No one at this hour pays attention to questions of toilette or personal elegance.

However, no one dreams of complaining of lack of comfort. All want to do their best to help the national cause in any way they can. The warmth of patriotic feeling is magnificent.

Already it is proposed to name streets in Paris after Samain, the young Alsatian who was shot in Metz for French sympathies, and after the cure of the frontier village who was murdered by German soldiers because he rang his church bells to give the alarm of their approach. Never did a nation rise to repel attack with a deeper resentment or a more vigorous *elan*.

One effect of the war has been to anathematize the name of Germany. The Villette district, through its local representatives, has presented a petition to the City Council praying that the name Rue d'Allemagne shall be changed to that of Rue Jean Jaures, in honor of the assassinated socialist leader.

Scenes of extraordinary enthusiasm marked the departure of the Fifth Regiment of Line from the Pepiniere barracks to-day. Long before six o'clock, the appointed hour of departure, the Avenue Portalis and the steps of the Church of Saint-Philippe du Roule were black with people.

At six o'clock the bugles sounded, the iron gates opened, and the regiment, with fixed bayonets, swung out into the road amid ringing cheers and shouts of "Vive la France!" As the standard-bearer passed, the cheer increased in volume, and men stood with bared heads and waved their hats in the air. The regiment entrained last night for the Belgian frontier.

Friday, August 7.

This is the sixth day of mobilization. Steady rain during the morning. Temperature at five P.M. 16 degrees centigrade.

Disembarking of British troops in France has begun, and the greatest enthusiasm is reported from the northern departments. I went to see the Duc de Loubet this morning and met there Mr. De Courcey Forbes, who told me that the French mobilization was working like clock-work two days ahead of scheduled time. He said that about a hundred Germans and Austrians had been arrested as spies. They were tried by court martial at eleven o'clock yesterday morning, and fifty-nine of them, who were found guilty, were shot at Vincennes at four o'clock the same afternoon.

It subsequently turned out that these spies had not been shot, after all, but had been imprisoned and kept in close confinement.

When Baron Schoen left the German Embassy in Paris, he was treated with great courtesy and escorted by the Chef de Protocol, M. William Martin, to the railway station, where he was provided with a special *train de luxe* with a restaurant car. Upon the arrival at the frontier, the Germans actually seized and confiscated the train! Reports of French families returning from Germany show that not only individual Frenchmen but French diplomatists and Russian diplomatists have been greatly insulted in Germany, especially in Berlin and Munich.

Contrast with this the attitude of a crowd which I saw to-day watching about a thousand Germans and Austrians tramp to a railway station, where they were entrained for their concentration camp. They marched between soldiers with fixed bayonets ready to protect them. But the crowd watched them almost sympathetically, with not an insult, not a jeer.

The mobilization in France has caused an extraordinary increase in the number of marriages contracted at the various Paris town halls. From morning till night the mayors and their assistants have been kept busy uniting couples who would be separated the same day or the next, when the husband joined his regiment. At the bare announcement of the possibility of war, the marriage offices at the town halls were literally taken by assault. As there was no time to be lost, arrangements were made by the chief officials to accept the minimum of documentary proofs of identity in all cases where the bridegrooms were called upon to serve their country. The other papers required by the law will be put in later.

The statistics of the first five days of the mobilization show that one hundred and eighty-one marriages were performed a day as against the ordinary figure of one hundred and ten. In the suburbs the increase is even greater, and a notable fact, both in Paris and outside, is that the largest number of marriages took place in the most populous districts. In the eleventh arrondissement the ordinary figures were trebled. All wedding parties wear little French, English, Russian, and Belgian flags.

General Michel, Military Governor of Paris, has issued an order formally forbidding any one to leave or enter Paris either on foot or in any kind of vehicle between the hours of six at night and six in the morning.

At a meeting of the executive committee of the American Ambulance of Paris, it was announced that more than thirty thousand francs had been received, exclusive of the sums obtained by the women's committee, and apart from the promises of larger subscriptions.

Up to yesterday morning twelve physicians and surgeons and twice that number of nurses had volunteered to assist the regular staff of the American Hospital in the work of caring for wounded French soldiers. Among the physicians and surgeons who have volunteered are Doctor Joseph Blake, of New York; Doctor Charles Roland, formerly a surgeon of the United States army; and Doctor George B. Hayes, of Paris.

The women's committee held a meeting at the American Embassy, when further subscriptions were received, that brought the total amount obtained by this committee up to eighteen thousand francs.

The executive committee now consists of Mrs. Laurence V. Benet, Mrs. H. Herman Harjes, Mrs. Potter Palmer, Mrs. Charles Carroll of Carrollton, Mrs. George Munroe, Mrs. Edith Wharton, Mrs. William Jay, Mrs. Tuck, Mrs. C.C. Cuyler and Mrs. Elbert H. Gary.

I was to-day with an American journalist who has an apartment in the Rue Hardy at Versailles. He is a single man, and his house is a fairly roomy one. The other day he was waited upon by a military officer, who told him that sixty thousand soldiers were to be billeted on the inhabitants--making one to every man, woman, and child in the city of the "Roi Soleil." They would need some part of his house--which, by the way, was formerly the domicile of Louis David, the great painter of Napoleon--and he would be glad if he could make arrangements to lodge four soldiers. My friend at once consented, and out of the five rooms he has kept two to himself. In the other three are billeted a cavalry officer and four soldiers. The only thing the American has had to complain of up to now is that every morning at six o'clock the officer wakes him up by playing the "Pilgrims' Chorus" from "Tannhauser" on the piano.

Germans are still found in strange places, considering the fact that the French are at war with them. I saw one man ask for his papers at the Gare de l'Est this afternoon, where with incredible assurance he was watching the entraining of French troops. He was led away between two policemen, and ought to feel thankful that the crowd did not get hold of him. He might have shared the same fate as that which befell one of his imprudent compatriots last Sunday at Clarendon. It was the day after mobilization had been declared, and the German knew that he must leave the country. But in a swaggering mood he said he would not leave until he had killed at least one of these condemned Frenchmen. His words were reported, and he fled into an entry and made his way into an adjoining house, where the crowd lost sight of him. When he emerged a cavalry escort protected him against the mad people who wanted to lynch him, and bundled him into a cab. He had been very badly handled, and his face was streaming with blood. He drove away as fast as the horse could gallop, but bystanders went after him, climbed up behind at the rear of the cab, and shot him dead through the little window.

Foreigners who know the women of France, who have lived in the country, have always given them a very high place as wives, mothers, and managers. But to-day they merit the admiration of the world more than ever.

I have seen them taking farewell of their husbands, sons, and brothers during the past few days, and nothing could surpass the courage with which they have sent them off to the war. They have struggled bravely to conceal their emotion, and only after the men have gone have the women given their feelings free play. An American lady who has seen some of these departures told me the other day that the sight of the children clinging to their fathers' hands so as to prevent them going away to the war was one of the saddest sights she had ever witnessed.

Saturday, August 8.

Seventh day of mobilization. Ideal summer weather. Temperature, 16 centigrade, with light westerly breezes. The moon is now full--a first-rate thing for the British fleet in search of German ships; also useful for French military operations, and for lighting the streets of Paris, thereby enabling economy in gas.

The news of the capture of Altkirch, in Alsace, by the French troops, reached Paris at about five o'clock this afternoon. It spread like wildfire through the city, and a rush was immediately made to buy the special editions of the newspapers announcing the victory.

To those who are not familiar with the Parisian character, the comparative silence with which the news was received came as a surprise. There was no enthusiastic outbreak of popular sentiment, no cheering, no throwing into the air of hats or sticks.

After forty-three years of weary waiting, the Tricolor floated over an Alsatian town. "At last!" That was the word that was heard on every side. The moment was too solemn to Frenchmen to allow them to say more.

The existence of war will be further brought home to Parisians on Monday by the disappearance of the morning breakfast rolls. In consequence of the great number of bakers now serving with the colors, it has been decided to simplify bread making in Paris so as to ensure the supply being regular, and consequently the only kinds obtainable after to-day will be those known as ***boulot*** and ***demi-fendu***.

The regulation of the milk supply is being rapidly organized. Those households in which milk is a necessity, for children, invalids, or the old, can obtain certificates giving them the preference. On the day after application for these certificates they are delivered, together with full particulars as to the amount, quantity, price, and place of purchase.

The position of other food supplies is excellent. The only difficulty is to get them delivered. Housekeepers must fetch their bread and milk if they want them to time.

Few articles of food have reached the maximum price laid down for them by the authorities. Fresh vegetables and fruit are very cheap. The only important articles which the shops have difficulty in supplying are sugar, condensed milk, and dried cereals.

During the past week about three thousand papers of nationality were issued at the American Consulate-general, and some sixteen hundred at the Embassy. This number may be taken as approximately coinciding with the number of American tourists now in Paris, as virtually all of these had to secure papers of nationality in order to register with the police.

Post-office regulations are still very strict. Following the discovery of numerous spies in and about Paris, General Michel has issued an order strictly prohibiting conversations on the telephone in any other language but French. When this order is not obeyed, the communication is immediately cut off.

Sunday, August 9.

Eighth day of mobilization. Hot summer day, with light southwesterly breezes. Temperature at five P. M. 26 degrees centigrade.

This may be regarded as the first Sunday of the war. Last Sunday was a day of rush and clamor in Paris. All shops were open and filled with eager customers; the streets were crammed with shouting crowds and hurrying vehicles; everything was forgotten in the outburst of national enthusiasm. In the afternoon and evening the city was the scene of riots and pillage.

To-day Paris presented a strong contrast. The news of French and Belgian successes at the front had cheered the hearts of Parisians, and, in spite of the strange aspect of the boulevards, denuded of their gay terraces, and of most of the ordinary means of locomotion, the city had something of a holiday aspect about it.

In the afternoon the city was crowded with promenaders dressed in Sunday garb. The proportion of women to men has largely increased, but the arrival of numerous reservists from the provinces caused Paris to appear, temporarily at least, somewhat less empty of men.

Indeed, the aspect of the city very much resembled that of any Sunday in summer, when the city is normally far from crowded.

I met MacAlpin of the *Daily Mail*, who said to me:

"I took a walk in the Bois de Boulogne yesterday afternoon. In a lonely alley I was stopped by three cyclist policemen. They asked for my papers. Fortunately, I had with me my passport and the 'permission to remain' issued to me as a foreigner. If I had happened to have left these in another coat, I should have been arrested.

"The policemen told me those were their orders. They added confidentially that they were looking for Germans. After this I saw many more cyclists on the same errand. They are hunting the woods systematically, because many Germans of suspicious character have taken refuge there.

"I rang up a friend on the telephone, and began, as usual: 'Hullo, is that you?' I was immediately told by the girl at the exchange that 'speaking in foreign languages was not permitted.' 'Unless you speak in French' she said, 'I shall cut you off at once.' I suppose she listened to what we were saying all the time.

"I went into a post-office to send a telegram to my wife. 'You must get it authorized at a police office' I was told. Not the simplest private message can be accepted until it has passed the censor."

No one is to be allowed from now on to have a complete wireless installation in Paris. Many people have set up instruments, some for amusement, some, it appears, for sinister purposes. No one may send messages now, though they are allowed to keep their receivers. In order to hear the messages which come through from Russia, the Eiffel Tower station, it is explained, needs "dead silence" in the air.

It was even announced two days ago that no one would be allowed to pass in or out of Paris between six at night and six in the morning. But this caused such inconvenience to so many people that the Military Governor of Paris was asked by the police to rescind his order, which he at once did.

The tenors and baritones and sopranos of the Opera and other theaters are going round singing in the courtyards for the benefit of the Red Cross. The Salon is turned into a military stable. Where the pictures hung, horses are munching their hay. The Comedie Francaise is to become a day nursery for the children of women who, in the absence of their husbands, are obliged to go out to work.

Mr. Herrick told me this afternoon that a few days ago the Telegraph Office refused his cipher cables to Washington. The Ambassador at once protested at the Ministry of Foreign Affairs, where the Minister, M. Doumergue, forthwith gave orders authorizing the telegraph office to accept his cipher messages. The Austrian Ambassador, who is still here, is not permitted to communicate by cipher telegrams with his Government. This is quite natural.

Monday, August 10.

Ninth day of mobilization. Hot, sunny weather. Temperature at five P.M. 29 degrees centigrade. Light southerly breeze.

Depicted on all faces this morning is anxious but confident expectation, for the public are conscious that a desperate encounter between two millions of men is impending in Belgium and on the Alsace-Lorraine border from Liege to Colmar.

The French capital is, at the present moment, a city of strange contrasts. Mothers, wives, sisters, and brides were last week red-eyed from the sorrow of parting. Now these same women have decorated their windows with bunting and have no thought other than of working as best they may to help the national cause.

In the streets, the shrill voices of children pipe the latest news from the front;

small girls cry grim details of the war.

All prisoners charged with light offenses who are mobilizable have been allowed to go to the front to rehabilitate themselves. The central prison of Fresnes, which ten days ago contained nine hundred criminals, has now only two hundred and fifty left.

And all the time Paris lives an every-day, humdrum life, makes the best of everything, and never complains.

Day by day the aspect of the streets becomes more normal, for the reason that more and more vehicles are freed from military service and can now resume their ordinary duties of transporting the public. Pending the return of the motor-omnibuses, a service of *char-a-bancs* has been started on the boulevards, which reminds Parisians of the days of the popular "Madeleine-Bastille" omnibus.

Diplomatic relations between France and Austria-Hungary were broken off to-day. War however has not been declared between France and Austria.

I met to-day M. Hedeman, the correspondent of the *Matin*, who recently witnessed in Berlin the arrival of Emperor William and the Crown Prince, which he compared to the departure of Napoleon III for Sedan in 1870. We were talking at the Ministry of War, where I also met the Marquis Robert de Flers, the well-known dramatist and editor of the *Figaro*, and M. Lazare Weiler, deputy. M. Hedeman told me that two days after the declaration of war a skirmish took place near the village of Genaville in the department of Meurthe-et-Moselle, between French custom-house officials and a squadron of German cavalry. The commander of the German detachment was shot in the stomach, fell to the ground, and was captured. He was Lieutenant Baron Marshall von Bieberstein, son of the former German Ambassador at Constantinople. A French lieutenant of gendarmes helped the prisoner to his feet. Lieutenant von Bieberstein, who was mortally wounded, said: "Thank you, gentlemen! I have done my duty in serving my country, just as you are serving your own!" He then died. M. Charles Humbert, senator of the Meuse, gave the helmet and sabre that had been worn by Lieutenant Marshall von Bieberstein to the editor of the *Matin*.

Tuesday, August 11.

Tenth day of mobilization. Warm, sunny weather, with light northerly breezes. Temperature at five P.M. 27 degrees centigrade.

Expectation of the great battle believed to be forthcoming to the north of Liege dominates the situation here.

I breakfasted to-day at the restaurant Paillard with M. Max-Lyon and M. Arthur Meyer, manager of the *Gaulois*. Mlle. Zinia Brozia, of the Opera Comique, who remains in Paris, was also of our party. All sorts of war rumors were current, but as M. Messimy, the minister of war, has given to M. Arthur Meyer the assurance that while the news given out "might not be *all* the news, it would nevertheless be invariably *true news*," confidence in the official communications to the press, which are the only authentic source of war news, is unshaken. The French Ministry of War, in its official *communique* of the military situation, issued at 11.30 this evening, states that the French troops are in contact with the enemy along almost the entire front. The only fighting that has taken place, however, has been engagements between the outposts, in which the French soldiers everywhere showed irresistible courage and ardor.

A Uhlan who was captured near Liege on Saturday was found to be the bearer of a map marked with the proposed marches of the German army. According to this map, the Germans were to be in Brussels on August 3 and at Lille on August 5.

Wednesday, August 12.

Eleventh day of mobilization. Hot weather, with light northerly breeze. Temperature at five P.M. 29 degrees centigrade.

Breakfasted with M. Galtier at the Cercle Artistique et Litteraire, Rue Volney. Several members of the club had just arrived from various watering-places. One of them, who came from Evian-les-Bains, said that he was sixty-two hours en route. The trains stop at every station so that they have uniform speed, thus rendering accidents almost out of the question. Only third-class tickets are sold, but these admit to all places.

It seems certain that the first part of the German plan--namely to come with a lightning-like, overwhelming crash through Belgium, via Liege and Namur--has failed. But the battle of millions along the vast front of two hundred and fifty miles between Liege and Verdun has opened, and the opposing armies are in touch with each other. Every one in Paris has confidence in the final result.

There is news of stupendous importance in the official announcement that Germany is employing the bulk of her twenty-six army corps against France and Belgium between Liege and Luxemburg. The disappearance of the German first line troops from the Russian frontier is now explained. By flinging this immense force upon France, Germany gains an advantage of numbers. How will she use it?

Paris seems to have seen very little, after all, of the mobilization. Most people may have seen an odd regiment pass, or perhaps numbers of horses obviously requisitioned. But they realize none of the feverish bustle of the mobilization centers.

Versailles relieves Paris of all this, and Versailles, since the first day of August, has been amazing. The broad avenues of the sleepy old town have been packed from side to side with men in uniform, men only partly in uniform, or men carrying their uniforms under their arm. At the first glance there seemed nothing but confusion, but the appearance was misleading, for at the Chantiers Station trainload after trainload of troops--men, guns, horses, material--have been despatched, taking the route of the Grande Ceinture Railway around Paris to Noisy-le-Sec, and on to the Est system.

At Versailles one realizes very fully that France is at war. For there are lines and lines of guns awaiting teams and drivers, hundreds upon hundreds of provision wagons, rows and rows of light draught-horses, many being shod in the street, while out along the road to Saint-Cyr, in a broad pasturage stretching perhaps half a mile, are thousands of magnificent cattle tightly packed together. They are to feed some of France's fighting force.

And at Saint-Cyr there is unheard-of activity. The second army flying corps is being organized. It consists of nearly eighty certificated volunteer pilots, including Garros, Chevillard, Verrier, Champel, Audemars, and many more well-known names. There are others than French airmen in the corps. Audemars is Swiss, while there are also an Englishman, a Peruvian, and a Dane. These men are all waiting eagerly the order to move.

Those at the American Embassy who are in charge of advancing funds to Americans in need of them had their busiest day since the work began, on Monday. Forty-six persons received a total of 3,514 francs.

The total amount of money distributed for the three days has been 8,869 francs. This has gone to 105 persons, which gives an average of the modest sum of 84 francs apiece, or less than seventeen dollars.

At least nine out of ten of the applicants are virtually without bankable credit of any kind. One man gave as security--because the money is advanced as a loan, not as a gift--a cheque on a Chicago bank, but he admitted that the cheque was not negotiable, as it was drawn on one of the Lorrimer banks of Chicago, which had gone into the hands of receivers since he left for Europe.

Callers included a number of negro song and dance artists who had come to the end of their resources.

The work of distributing money is entirely in the hands of American army officers, and they investigate every case which has not already been investigated by the relief committee appointed by the Ambassador. Major Spencer Cosby, the military attache at the Embassy, is the treasurer of the fund. Investigations are made by Captain Frank Parker, assisted by Lieutenants William H. Jouett and H. F. Loomis. The cashier is Captain Francis H. Pope, with Lieutenants Francis W. Honeycutt and B.B. Somervell as assistants.

When the history of the great war is written, a very honorable place will have to be reserved for the women of Paris. In the work of caring for the destitute and unemployed of their own sex, and anticipating the needs of great numbers of wounded men, they are showing extraordinary energy. Every day new and special philanthropic institutions are started and carried on by women in Paris.

Comtesse Greffulhe has taken in hand the provision of food and lodging for convalescent soldiers, so as to relieve the pressure on public and private hospitals and ambulances. Mme. Couyba, wife of the Minister of Labor, is arranging for the supply of free food to girls and women out of work. Marquise de Dion, Mme. Le Menuet and other ladies are opening temporary workshops where women can obtain employment at rates that will enable them to tide over the hard times before them.

The Union des Femmes de France is doing wonderful work in the organization of hospitals and in sending out nurses to wherever they are most likely to be needed.

One of the finest examples of energy and devotion is being set by the wife of the Military Governor of Paris, Mme. Michel. She has identified herself specially with what may be briefly described as "saving the babies." Her idea is to see that the coming generation shall not be sacrificed and that expectant mothers whose natural defenders have gone to the war shall not feel themselves forsaken.

Mme. Michel is the president of a committee of ladies who have undertaken, each in her own district, to seek out needy mothers, to see that they and their children receive assistance, and to give them all possible moral support.

Mme. Michel is putting in about eighteen hours' work a day in the discharge of her duties. She is up at daylight, and after dealing with a mass of correspondence, is out in her motor-car before seven o'clock, on a round of the various *mairies*, to see that the permanent maternity office, which it has been found necessary to start in every one of these municipal centers, is doing its work properly.

At eleven o'clock she is back at the big house which is the official residence of her husband, close to the Invalides, and is presiding over a committee meeting. She lunches in about a quarter of an hour, and plunges into more committee work, which usually lasts until well after four o'clock.

The latter part of the afternoon is taken up in another tour of inspection, dinner is a movable feast to be observed if there happens to be time for it, and then there is another pile of letters and telegrams a foot high to be gone through and answered; and so to bed, very late.

Thursday, August 13.

Twelfth day of mobilization. Hot, sultry weather with faint northeasterly wind. Thermometer at five P.M. 30 degrees centigrade.

Breakfasted to-day at the restaurant Paillard and met there M. Arthur Meyer, M. Max-Lyon, Maitre Charles Philippe of the French Bar, and Mr. Slade, manager of the Paris branch of the Equitable Trust Company. War! War! War! was the subject of the conversation, but no real news from the front except of outpost fighting, with success for the French and the Belgians. Gabriele d'Annunzio's flaming "Ode for the Latin Resurrection," published to-day in the *Figaro*, is evidently intended to excite Italians to seize an opportunity to abandon neutrality and join France and the Allied Powers against Austria, and thereby win back the "Italia Irredenta." D'Annunzio invokes the Austrian oppression of bygone days in Mantua and Verona, calls Austria the "double-headed Vulture," and summons all true Italians to take the war-path of revenge. "Italy! Thine hour has struck for Barbarians call thee to arms! *Vae Victis!* Remember Mantua!"

After lunch I met Mrs. Edith Wharton, who had made some valuable mental and written notes of what she has seen in Paris. She is about to leave for England.

So sure were the Germans of advancing rapidly into France that they had decided to complete their mobilization on French territory. According to the *Figaro*, an Alsatian doctor, who came to France on the outbreak of hostilities, had been ordered to join the German army at Verdun on the third day of mobilization. A German tailor, living in Paris, had instructions to join at Rheims on the thirteenth day.

Although the early closing hour of all cafes and restaurants causes some inconvenience, it is being taken in good part by Parisians. It has not the slightest effect on the habits of the city as far as keeping late hours is concerned--no power on earth could make the Parisian go to bed at nine o'clock.

People cannot spend their evenings in the cafes, so they spend them either strolling or sitting about in the streets, smoking and chatting for hours. But the new closing hour has had the effect expected by the authorities. It has made Paris the most orderly city in the world. The police are, however, kept very busy, for the regulation as to carrying papers is being rigorously enforced, and the belated pedestrian is invariably challenged by a cavalry patrol or by the ordinary police. If his answers are unsatisfactory, he undergoes a more searching examination at the police station.

Paris has become a paradise for cyclists. Owing to the lack of transportation facilities, hundreds of Parisians have taken to using bicycles as a practical mode of locomotion, and the city now swarms with them. This state of things is not, however, likely to last very long, for every day brings more vehicles back to the capital, and every day brings a further step towards a more normal situation.

Some cars requisitioned will hardly be returned,--as is evidenced by the experience of Mrs. Julia Newell and her sister, Miss Josephine Pomeroy, two Americans just returned to Paris.

Before the war broke out, Miss Pomeroy left Frankfort by automobile, but in passing through Metz her $5,000 Delaunay-Belleville machine was confiscated by the Germans, and her footman and chauffeur, who were Frenchmen, were put into prison. All her luggage was lost. No attention was paid to her protests that she was an American citizen.

Friday, August 14.

Thirteenth day of mobilization. Another hot, stifling day with thermometer (centigrade) 31 degrees at five P.M.

Lunched at the Cercle Artistique et Litteraire, Rue Volney. Only the old servants remain. The club is no longer open to non-member dinner guests. The price of meals is reduced to three and a half francs for lunch, and to four francs for dinner, including wine, mineral water, beer, or cider. There is great scarcity of small change. To alleviate this, ivory bridge or poker counters, marked fifty *centimes*, and one *franc*, are given in change and circulate for payment of meals, drinks, etc.

Greater military activity is noticed in the streets than for some days past. Many movements of troops took place all day, and long convoys of the ambulance corps, including several complete field hospital staffs, were seen driving and marching through the city.

This was due to the fact that within the last few days large bodies of the territorial forces had concentrated in the environs, notably at Versailles, from whence they left for the front.

Early this morning certain districts of Paris literally swarmed with soldiers of the territorial reserve.

Although most of them are married men and fathers, they display as fine a spirit as their younger comrades. They may, perhaps, show less enthusiasm, but that they are quite as calm is shown by the fact that a number of them spent the last hours before their departure fishing in the Ourcq Canal.

A detachment of naval reserves has been brought to Paris to assist the police and the Municipal Guards in assuring order in the capital. The men wear the uniform of *fusiliers marins*, and correspond to the marines in the British navy. They will be placed under the orders of the Prefect of Police.

Mr. A. Beaumont of the ***Daily Telegraph*** has had a very narrow escape from being shot as a spy. He is a naturalized American citizen, but was born in Alsace. When the present war broke out, he started in a motor-car to the front without the necessary passes and permits. He circulated about and obtained good and useful news for his paper. The other day, however, he was brought to a standstill in Belgium and was arrested. The Belgian authorities asked at the French headquarters: "What shall we do with him?" The reply was: "Send him on here to headquarters, and if he proves to be a spy he will be court-martialed and shot." This arose from the confusion of names. It seems that the doings of a German spy named Bremont, of Alsatian birth, had become known to the military authorities in France and Belgium. Beaumont stoutly asserted that he was the victim of mistaken identity, and only after very great difficulty, and with the exceptional efforts of Mr. Herrick and of Sir Francis Bertie, the British Ambassador, was he able to establish his true identity, when he was released by the French Headquarter Staff, and handed over to the Ministry of Foreign Affairs.

Arrivals of detachments of German prisoners continue to be reported from various parts of France. A Prussian officer, speaking French fluently, was among a convoy of prisoners at Versailles yesterday. The officer, on seeing some French territorials march past, singing the "Marseillaise," remarked to his guard: "What a disillusion awaits us!"

Saturday, August 15.
(*Feast of the Assumption.*)

Fourteenth day of mobilization. Heavy thunder storms set in at three A.M. Showers followed until one o'clock; cloudy afternoon with variable wind. Thermometer at five P.M. 22 degrees centigrade.

Huge crowds lined the streets leading from the Gare du Nord to the British Embassy, to welcome Field-marshal Sir John French, Commander of the British expeditionary force, who came to visit President Poincare before taking command of his army. At quarter to one, three motor-cars rapidly approached the Embassy. In the second I could get a glimpse of Sir John in his gray-brown khaki uniform. His firm, trim appearance and his clear blue eyes, genial smile, and sunburnt face made an excellent impression, and he was greeted with loud cheers. He had a long talk with M. Messimy, Minister of War.

I am having a very busy time trying to obtain permission for American war correspondents to accompany the French armies in the field. Mr. Richard Harding

Davis and Mr. D. Gerald Morgan have arrived in London on the **Lusitania** from New York to act as war correspondents in the field with the French forces. As president of the Association of the Foreign Press, and as Paris correspondent of the **New York Tribune**, I made special applications at the Ministry of Foreign Affairs and at the War Office for authority for them to act as war correspondents for the **New York Tribune**. These applications were endorsed by Ambassador Herrick, who also did everything possible to secure permission for them to take the field.

The official regulations for war correspondents are much more severe, however, than those enforced during the Japanese and Turkish wars. In the first place, only Frenchmen and correspondents of one of the belligerent nationalities, that is to say French, British, Russian, Belgian, or Servian, are allowed to act as war correspondents. Frenchmen may represent foreign papers. All despatches must be written in the French language and must be sent by the military post, and only after having been formally approved by the military censor. No despatches can be sent by wire or by wireless telegraphy. No correspondent can circulate in the zone of operations unless accompanied by an officer especially designated for that purpose. All private as well as professional correspondence must pass through the hands of the censor. War correspondents of whatever nationality will, during their sojourn with the army, be subject to martial law, and if they infringe regulations by trying to communicate news not especially authorized by the official censors, will be dealt with by the laws of espionage in war time. These are merely a few among the many rigid prescriptions governing war correspondents.

I talked with several editors of Paris papers on the subject, notably with M. Arthur Meyer of the **Gaulois**, Marquis Robert de Flers of the **Figaro**, and M. Georges Clemenceau of the **Homme Libre**. They one and all expressed the opinion that war correspondents would enjoy exceptional opportunities, enabling them to get mental snap-shots of picturesque events and to acquire valuable first-hand information for writing magazine articles or books, but that from a newspaper standpoint there would be insurmountable difficulties preventing them from getting their "news to market," that is to say, in getting their despatches on the wires for their respective papers. However, Mr. Herrick is doing everything he can to obtain all possible facilities for Mr. Davis and for Mr. Morgan.

Almost every day brings some fresh measure in the interest of the public. Yesterday the Prefect of Police issued an order forbidding the sale of absinthe in the cafes under pain of immediate closure, and again called the attention of motorists to the regulations which they are daily breaking.

The sanitary authorities, too, have their hands full. So far, however, the present circumstances have had no influence on the state of health in Paris. The weekly bulletin published by the municipality shows that the death and disease figures are quite normal.

Mr. Bernard J. Schoninger, chairman of the committee which has recently been formed by the American Chamber of Commerce in Paris with the object of settling difficult questions which may arise in Franco-American commercial relations, states that his committee is collaborating with the ladies' committee founded by the wife of the American Ambassador to assist wounded soldiers. In a few days this committee collected one hundred and seventy-five thousand francs. His own committee has issued an appeal to all Chambers of Commerce in the United States, and he trusts that considerable funds will be forthcoming for the ambulance corps created under the auspices of the American Hospital in Paris. The Minister for War has granted the use of the Lycee Pasteur, where it is hoped to establish an ambulance of two hundred beds, which may later be increased to one thousand.

The committee has also taken up the question of the payment of customs duties on American imports into France, and Mr. Schoninger states that he has met with the greatest kindness and that the French customs authorities have agreed to accept guarantees from various commercial syndicates instead of actual immediate cash payments. This will obviate difficulties occasioned by the refusal of French banking establishments, acting under the terms of the moratorium, in handing over funds which they have on deposit.

Sunday, August 16.

Fifteenth day of mobilization. Gray, cloudy day with occasional showers and westerly wind. Thermometer at five P.M. 17 degrees centigrade.

I drove out in the Bois de Boulogne after lunch with the Duc de Loubat. The Bois was rather deserted; only a few couples were strolling about or seated on benches reading newspapers. Went to the Cercle des Patineurs, where fences were being put up on the lawns to enclose sheep and oxen to provision Paris. In the tennis court we saw about two hundred Kabyles from Algeria, who had been found astray in Paris. They sleep on straw beds in the tennis court and are provided with rations. They are all men, and will be drafted into the Algerian reserves.

Madame Waddington, formerly Miss King of New York, and widow of the late William Henry Waddington, senator, and member of several French Cabinets, and one of the French delegates to the Berlin Conference in 1878, remains in Paris, and is stopping with her sister, Miss King, at her apartment in the Rue de La Tremouille. Madame Waddington was a great friend of the late King Edward VII, who never passed through Paris without calling to see her and lunching with her and her family. Madame Waddington, who is in excellent health and spirits, told me that the feeling was so strong against the Austro-Hungarian Ambassador, Count Szecsen de Temerin, during the last few days of his stay here after hostilities had begun with Germany, that one evening, as he was about to sit down to dinner with his fellow diplomatist, M. Alexandre Lahovary, the Roumanian Minister, at the Cercle de l'Union, which is one of the most select and restricted clubs of Paris, the secretary of the club requested M. Lahovary to announce to the Austrian Ambassador that the committee of the club expressed the wish that he should no longer take his meals at the club nor appear on the premises, because his presence under prevailing political conditions rendered the Austrian Ambassador an "undesirable personage." The Austrian Ambassador, who had just ordered an excellent bottle of Mouton Rothschild claret for his dinner, at once left the club.

Parisians flocked in thousands to-day to the basilica of the Sacre Coeur of Montmartre, where special services were held. This church was planned and built in expiation of the war of 1870. It was finished only a few months ago, and was to have been definitely "inaugurated" next month.

A detachment of about four thousand men of the Naval Reserve, most of whom are Bretons, is encamped to the north of Paris at Le Bourget, and there have been stirring scenes in the little church there. It has been crowded with sailors and soldiers at every service, for Bretons are among the most religious of all peoples of France.

Abbe Marcade, the cure of Le Bourget, has had magnificent congregations. On the Feast of the Assumption the Abbe decided to hold Mass in the open air. An altar was accordingly set up in a large field beside a haystack. Thirty-five hundred soldiers attended. At the end, the Abbe, standing on a table, preached a sermon in the falling rain.

These military services at Le Bourget have been strikingly picturesque. The Abbe's sermons are interrupted from time to time by cheers, as if he were making a political speech. His words on patriotism and soldiers' duty have been greeted with shouts of "Vive la France." Loudest of all was the applause when he declared that feelings of party were now drowned in love for the country. In the evening, after the service at which this sermon was preached, the Abbe dined with the officers of the regiment and with the socialist mayor of the commune, a thing which would have been impossible in ordinary times. The war has made Frenchmen stand together in closer unity than they have ever done before.

One of the strangest changes brought about by the war is that of the fashionable race-courses of Auteuil and Longchamp. These have been turned into large grazing farms for sheep and cattle requisitioned by the military authorities. Another curious requisition is that of all French military uniforms in the wardrobes of the Paris theaters.

Mobilization orders to rejoin his regiment at Rheims on August 7 have been found in the possession of a wounded German soldier in hospital at Brussels. The man stated that several of his comrades had received orders to join the colors at other French towns on specified dates. This shows how the German plans were upset by the resistance at Liege.

Field-marshal Sir John French slept at the British Embassy last night, and after a rousing reception left Paris at seven o'clock this morning in an automobile for an "unknown destination."

Every man in France is envying the young dragoon officer, Lieutenant Bruyant, who has been given the first Cross of the Legion of Honor in the war. The lieutenant with six men was scouting near the frontier, when suddenly he saw a number of horsemen moving a good way off, and made them out to be a patrol of twenty-seven Uhlans. Shots were exchanged and a German fell. Then the Uhlans cantered away. They were four to one, but did not care to fight.

The French followed up resolutely, but the Germans kept their distance. When the dragoons trotted, the Uhlans trotted too. Now the former would gallop across a bit of open country, and the Germans would gallop away just as quickly. Evidently they were making for shelter.

Soon Lieutenant Bruyant saw that they were trying to reach a wood, where they could take cover. No time was to be lost. He knew that if they got there they would escape him. Now was the moment to unchain the ardor of his men. He gave the orders "Draw swords!" "Charge!"

The seven spurred their horses and fell upon the twenty-seven with shouts of defiance. The shock demoralized the Germans, who made no stand at all. One was killed by a lance thrust. The officer in command was drawing his revolver when Lieutenant Bruyant cut him down with his sabre. Six more were wounded and knocked off their horses. The rest fled in disorder.

Monday, August 17.

Sixteenth day of mobilization. Gray, cloudy weather with northerly breezes. Thermometer at five P.M. 17 degrees centigrade.

The first trophy of the war, the flag of the One Hundred and Thirty-second German Infantry Regiment (First Regiment of Lower Alsace), arrived in Paris this morning, having been brought by motor-car from the front, where it was captured at Sainte-Blaise by the Tenth Battalion of Chasseurs-a-Pieds (riflemen), a corps which distinguished itself in the Franco-Austrian war of 1859 by capturing the first Austrian flag at Solferino. In 1840, the Tenth Chasseurs-a-Pied were commanded by Patrice de MacMahon, then a major and afterwards Marshal of France and Duc de Magenta, and whose name is remembered by the corps in their march song:

"L' dixiem' batallion,
Commandant Mac-Mahon,
N'a pas peur du canon,
Nom de nom!"

The captured flag is of magenta colored silk, with a white St. Andrew's cross, on which the imperial eagle and the regimental insignia are embroidered in gold. The news that a German flag was being shown spread rapidly, and a large crowd gathered. There were no insulting remarks, merely quiet observation. Among the first to see the trophy were some school-children headed by their master, who explained the significance of the capture. The flag was taken to the Elysee Palace and shown to President Poincare, who is himself a major of chasseurs-a-pied. It was afterwards placed in the Invalides.

General Michel, the Governor of Paris, has notified all places of public entertainment that their programmes must henceforth be submitted to the censors under pain of closure of the establishment.

Except for trifling drawbacks, inevitable in times like the present, Paris has little to complain of. There are everywhere signs of a gradual return to normal conditions. Among these is the reappearance of flowers on the costermongers' carts and at the kiosks. In the early stages of the mobilization, when many thousands of families were saying good-by to their men, no one had the heart to buy flowers, even had any supply been available. The conveyance to Paris of flowers grown in the neighborhood of the capital has now been reorganized, and roses and carnations are being sold on the main thoroughfares at normal prices.

Women and girl newspaper-sellers have become familiar figures in Paris, and their number is increasing steadily as the needs of the army are depriving more and more families of their bread-winners. A pathetic figure seen on the Boulevard des Italiens yesterday afternoon was a woman toiling along under the weight of a sleeping child about five years old, and calling her newspapers gently, so as not to wake him.

Tuesday, August 18.

Seventeenth day of mobilization. Cloudy weather with occasional patches of blue sky. Thermometer at five P.M. 17 degrees centigrade. Light northeasterly wind.

It is now for the first time officially announced that the British expeditionary force has safely landed in France and in Belgium. The transportation has been effected in perfect order, promptly on schedule time, and without the slightest hitch or casualty. British troops were everywhere received with immense enthusiasm. Not only have they landed at Ostend, Boulogne, and Havre, with all their field transports, but they have been taken up the Seine in steamers to Rouen, whence they were entrained on the strategic lines for Belgium. M.J.A. Picard, a young Frenchman, and his wife arrived from New York and reached Paris via Boulogne.

M. Picard will join the army to-morrow as a reservist employed in the general staff. His wife will act as a correspondent of the **Tribune** in France. M. Picard said that Boulogne was full of British troops. They marched through the narrow streets of the city wearing their khaki uniforms, thousands upon thousands of them, roaring as they pass the new British war slogan: "Are we downhearted? *No-o-o-o! Shall we win? Ye-e-e-e-s-s-s!*" Then came an Irish regiment with their brown jolly faces beaming with fun, and singing: "It's a long way to Tipperary ... It's a long way to go!" A Welsh battalion followed, whistling the "Marseillaise." The prettiest girls in every town throw flowers and kisses to these stalwart British lads. As soon as the order to break ranks is given, bevies of smiling lasses surround the troops, offering them sandwiches, fruit, wine, and flowers, and even kisses. There would be thousands of jealous girls in England, Scotland, Ireland, and Wales to-day if they could but witness the reception. Highland regiments wearing the kilt have stupendous success with the blushing young women of France.

From the seat of war in Belgium, and also in the North Sea, the same awful silence continues, and Parisians manifest growing impatience for the inevitable great battle. I went to the Ministry of War with M. and Mme. Picard, but no news of military importance was communicated.

Wednesday, August 19.

Eighteenth day of mobilization. Fine summer weather, with light northerly wind. Temperature at five P.M. 17 degrees centigrade.

Absolute silence concerning military movements in Belgium. No official communication was made to-day at the Ministry of War. Parisians feel that momentous events are about to take place but look forward with calm confidence.

I called upon my old friend, M. Rene Baschet, manager of the **Illustration**, which is the only illustrated weekly paper in France to continue its issue. I hastened to tell M. Baschet that I had received a private telegram from Rome announcing that the Pope was so ill that his physicians, and above all Monseigneur Zampini, did not think that His Holiness could live through the night. M. Baschet paid genuine tribute to Lord Kitchener's instructions "to every soldier of the British expeditionary forces," and said that the British War Minister showed himself at once "heroic and hygienic," and cited the passage: "You may find temptations, both in wine and women. You must entirely resist both temptations, and while treating all women with perfect courtesy, you should avoid any intimacy."

At the Ministry of Foreign Affairs, I met M. Jules Cambon, French Ambassador at Berlin, who after being treated discourteously by the Germans and dealt with practically as a prisoner, reached Paris by way of Denmark and England. It would have been indiscreet to ask M. Jules Cambon to disclose diplomatic secrets, but after conversing with persons who accompanied him, it seems certain that there had been complete understanding between Germany and Austria about the sending of Austria's ultimatum to Servia. It is true that German diplomacy had not accepted the exact terms of the ultimatum communicated to Servia on July 23 and had asked for certain modifications in the text, which Austria refused to make. M. Cambon drew an important distinction between German ***diplomacy***, and the German ***military clique***. The former were willing only to go so far as ***risking*** a war, while the latter seized the opportunity to ***bring on*** the war and to attack France. The discussion lasted two or three days, and the military caste, receiving the strong personal encouragement and support of Emperor William, became omnipotent, and from that moment war was inevitable. In regard to France, Germany constantly repeated the formula: "Put strong pressure upon Russia, your ally, to prevent her from helping the Servians!" To this France replied: "Very good, but you yourself should put strong pressure upon Austria, your ally, to prevent her from provoking a catastrophe!" To this Germany rejoined: "Ah! But that is not the same thing!" Thus it was in this "***cercle vicieux***" that the diplomatic conversation continued, which, under the circumstances, and especially owing to the attitude of Emperor William, could end in nothing else but war.

Thursday, August 20.

Nineteenth day of mobilization. Ideal summer weather. Light northerly breezes. Temperature at five P.M. 16 degrees centigrade.

Good news of further French advances in Upper Alsace and the recapture of Muelhausen make Parisians cheerful. The death of the Pope during the present tension is scarcely noticed. All thoughts and expectations are centered on Belgium, where the great battle is impending.

It is announced at the Ministry of War that it was not the Tenth but the First

Battalion of Chasseurs-a-Pied that captured the German regimental flag now hung in the Invalides. The French tobacco factories are working night and day to supply the armies with tobacco, for in all countries soldiers and sailors are ardent devotees to "My Lady Nicotine." In honor of the Belgians, a special cigarette, *La Liegeoise*, has been produced, which is naturally tipped with cork (*liege*). The stock of "Virginia" has run short for supply to the British soldiers. The "Virginia," being slightly scented, is known in France as *tabac a la confiture*, but large quantities are being imported from Liverpool expressly to satisfy Tommy Atkins.

I met at the War Office, M. Pegoud, inventor of "looping the loop," who was being congratulated by M. Messimy, Minister of War. He came here to get a new aeroplane, his own having been riddled through the wings by ninety-seven bullets and two shells when he was making a raid of one hundred and eighty miles into German territory. He naturally did not tell me *where* he went, but simply said he crossed the Rhine with an official observer and blew up, by means of bombs, two German convoys. "Captain Fink," he stated, "destroyed the Frascati airship shed near Metz, where there was a Zeppelin which was wrecked. He also destroyed three Taube aeroplanes, which were also in the shed."

General Bonnal, formerly professor of strategy at the Ecole Militaire, says: "The greatest piece of good fortune for France that can be expected, is that Emperor William will take personal command of all the German armies. This is now an accomplished fact, and it gives us all immense encouragement."

Friday, August 21.

Twentieth day of mobilization. Threatening weather with overcast sky. Northwesterly wind. Temperature at five P.M. 19 degrees centigrade. No clouds prevented the eclipse of the sun from being seen in Paris. Most people however were profoundly indifferent to the celestial phenomena.

Thousands of foreign volunteers assembled on the Esplanade des Invalides this morning to offer their services for the war. These young foreigners are mostly strong, active youths and have all received more or less military training. They marched through the streets in detachments of from two to six hundred, grouped together according to nationalities, bearing French flags alongside flags of their own countries. There were about five thousand Russians, five thousand Italians, two thousand Belgians, numerous Czecs, Slavs, Roumanians, and Armenians, together with smaller contingents of Americans, British, and Greeks. Mr. Arthur Bles and his second in command, Mr. Victor Little, are busy organizing the "Rough Riders" in a riding-school in Rue Avenue des Chasseurs.

M. Geissler, manager of the Hotel Astoria, who was recently reported as having been shot as a spy for arranging disks on the roof of his hotel to interfere with the French wireless telegraphy, was tried today, not by court martial, but by a civil judge, M. Tortat, to whom the court martial had referred the matter for further evidence. It appears that M. Geissler had been denounced on insufficient grounds by a clerk in his employment. His innocence was established, this morning, and he was released from the Sante prison and handed over to the military authorities, who will probably let the matter drop.

Saturday, August 22.

Mobilization is now completed. This is the nineteenth day since the declaration of war (August 3). A sultry day with light northwesterly breezes. Thermometer at five P.M. 22 degrees centigrade.

"All that I can say to you is that the battle has begun. That is all I know," is the statement made by M. Malvy, Minister of the Interior, as he stepped into his motor-car at the Elysee Palace on his way home this evening after the meeting of the Council of National Defence. Remarkable, impressive silence prevails everywhere. If people speak, it seems to be in a whisper. Never before was Paris so full of motor-ambulances, all driving hurriedly hither and thither, bearing nurses or Red Cross attendants, but never a wounded. The whole of the Rue Francois-Premier is lined on both sides with Red Cross motor-cars. The railway stations have an unusual appearance, with hundreds of wooden booths forming a sort of barrier to approaches. The calm, confident, silent, patriotic expectation augurs well for the future and vividly contrasts with the noisy, braggadocio spirit of 1870. Paris at the present moment is the most orderly, well-behaved city in the world.

I met at the Cafe Napolitain, a favorite resort of journalists, my friend Laurence Jerrold, chief Paris correspondent of the **London Daily Telegraph**. We spoke of the stories showing the amazing ignorance in which German officers have been kept regarding the situation. Mr. Jerrold told me that a relative of his, who is a

French officer, saw yesterday two Prussian lieutenants, who, as prisoners of war, were being taken around Paris, to a town in western France. Both spoke French perfectly. At Juvisy station, where the train stopped, they said to the French officer: "Of course, we know why you are taking us around Paris and not ***into*** Paris. Paris is in a state of revolution, and you don't want us to see what is going on there." Argument followed; the Prussian officers persisted that Paris was in revolt, that France stood alone, that England had declared neutrality, that an Italian army had already crossed the French frontier and had invaded the department of Haute Savoie, etc. The French officer rushed to the waiting-room, bought all the newspapers he could find, and brought them back to the Prussian prisoners, who fell aghast and read them in silence, as the train proceeded.

The curator of the Louvre Museum has taken every possible precaution to ensure the safety of the works of art under his care. The Venus of Milo has been placed in a strong-room lined with steel plates--a sort of gigantic safe--and stands in absolute security from any stray Zeppelin bombs. The Winged Victory of Samothrace is also protected by armor plates. Mona Lisa once more smiles in darkness. The Salle Greque, containing masterpieces of Phidias, is protected by sand bags. Many unique treasures of statuary and painting are placed in the cellars. Similar precautions are taken at the Luxembourg and at other museums. The upper stories of the Louvre, which are roofed in glass, are being converted into hospital wards, and thus the collections of the national museum, which belong to all time and to all nations, enjoy the protection of the Red Cross flag.

I made a brief trip to Versailles, which has been transformed into an arsenal and a vast supply depot for food and forage. Troops of the military commissariat train are cantoned in the parks and shooting preserves of Prince Murat and of Mr. James Gordon Bennett. The attractive little summer residence of Miss Elsie de Wolff and Miss Elizabeth Marbury is occupied by cavalry officers. Versailles is the mobilization center or assembly for the southwestern military regions, and over fifty thousand men have been equipped here and sent on to their destinations at the front. Herds of cattle and flocks of sheep are grazing contentedly on the lawns and meadows of the chateau.

The membership of the executive committee of the women's committee of the American Ambulance has been increased by the addition of Mrs. Robert Woods

Bliss, Mrs. Cooper Hewitt, and Mrs. Barton French.

Among the American women who have volunteered to serve as nurses in the hospital now being established in the Lycee Pasteur, in Neuilly, are the following: Mrs. H. Herman Harjes, Mrs. Frederick H. Allen, Mrs. Laurence V. Benet, Mrs. Whitney Warren, Mrs. Charles Carroll, Miss Ives, Miss Edith Deacon, Mrs. Barton French and Miss Treadwell.

Sunday, August 23.

Twenty-first day of the war. A hot sultry day, with southerly wind. Temperature at five P.M. 25 degrees centigrade.

The fourth Sunday of August finds Paris silently awaiting news from the great battle going on for a distance of one hundred and five miles extending from Mons to the Luxemburg frontier, and which is expected to rage for several days. Parisians receive with enthusiasm the news communicated by M. Iswolski, the Russian Ambassador, announcing that three of the five army corps which Germany has in East Prussia have been defeated by the army of General Rennekampf, near Gumbinnen.

I drove to-day with the Duke de Loubat, who is a close friend of Cardinal Ferrata, now spoken of as foremost favorite among the *Papabili* Cardinals. Monseigneur Ferrata enjoys great popularity not only at Rome but abroad, and is a warm friend of the United States. He has also a keen sense of humor. Not long ago a distinguished member of the French parliament lunched with Monseigneur Ferrata and remarked: "How is it that the Church requires such a long lapse of time before pronouncing a decree of nullity of marriage?" "Well," replied Cardinal Ferrata, "before the end of the ten years' delay, it is usually found that *one of the three* dies or disappears, and that the petition consequently is no longer pressed!" A great change is noticeable in the Paris churches. They have been more crowded since the war than for many years past. I entered the Madeleine to-day and found, to my surprise, an unusually large proportion of men among the congregation. Most of them were reservists called to arms. In other churches the congregations were almost entirely composed of women and children.

Our Ambassador, Herrick, is a sort of guardian angel for Americans in Paris. I saw him to-day working with Mr. Robert Woods Bliss, first secretary of the Embassy. He rose at six in the morning, and except for a brief repose for breakfast and dinner, is constantly ready to give advice to Americans or to attend to intricate diplomatic duties that crop up here at every turn. Our Ambassador also has on his shoulders the affairs of all the Germans and Austrians who remain in France. Some of our countrymen are very hard to please. Everything possible is being done for those who wish to return home, and money, when necessary, is advanced to them for the purpose. But they strongly object to waiting in line for their turn, whether at the Embassy, the Consulate, or at the Transatlantic Company, where, owing to the crowd of applicants, there is some necessary delay in attending to them.

A number of complications have arisen by discharged servants filing statements against their former employers, denouncing them as "probable spies." Several examples of this have already occurred with prominent American ladies who permanently reside here. I spoke with M. Hennion, the prefect of police, on the subject, and he said that "such malicious accusations"--and he showed me a pile of denunciations nearly a yard high--"were never acted upon, unless under *really suspicious circumstances*."

One of Mr. Herrick's callers at the American Embassy was Mme. Henri de Sincay, a grand-daughter of General Logan, of Civil War fame. She is the wife of a French army officer and when the war broke out was living in a chateau near Liege. She fled to Brussels with her child, and then, leaving the latter there with her sister-in-law, came to Paris to say good-by to her husband, who is attached to the aviation corps near Versailles. Now Mme. de Sincay cannot return to her child, but she is not worrying over the situation and has offered her services to the American Ambulance here in Paris.

The earnest, practical way in which General Victor Constant Michel, Military Governor of Paris, carries out his work, is admirable. General Michel has quietly despatched large numbers of the unruly youths of Belleville, Montmartre, and Montparnasse,--known as the "apaches"--to the country, in small gangs, to reap the wheat harvest, and he also employs them in the government cartridge and ammunition factories. In Paris, they have completely vanished from sight. The prohibition of the drinking and sale of absinthe, not only in Paris, but throughout France, was also due to the foresight of the Military Governor. General Michel, although a rigid disciplinarian and a masterful organizer, is extremely affable and agreeable.

He was born at Auteuil in 1850, and after graduation from Saint-Cyr, the French West Point, served in the war of 1870-1871 as second lieutenant of infantry. In 1894 he was made colonel of an infantry regiment and showed such proficiency during the manoeuvers that he became general-of-brigade in 1897. He was made general-of-division in 1902; he is member of the Supreme War Council, and in 1910 was awarded the high distinction of Grand Officer of the Legion of Honor.

Monday, August 24.

Twenty-second day of the war. Hot day with bright blue sky and southeasterly wind. Thermometer at five P.M. 27 degrees centigrade.

Terrific night and day fighting continues on the Sambre and Meuse. The French attack seems to have been repulsed. The allies remain on the defensive, awaiting further German attacks. The losses on both sides are terrible. Some days yet must elapse before the final result of the great battle can be known. Meanwhile, Paris waits with patriotic confidence. Russian victories in East Prussia, the Japanese bombardment of Tsin-Tao, in Kiao-Chow, the advance of the Servians, and the increasing probability of Italy claiming eventually her "*irredenta*" territory, are all encouraging factors in this world-wide war.

The American volunteers mustered to-day at their recruiting offices in the Rue de Valais and marched to the Invalides, where they passed the French medical test prior to enrolment in the French army. The men are wonderfully fit, and their splendid muscular, wiry physique was greatly admired as they marched through the streets. Out of the two hundred present, only one was not passed by the army surgeons, and even he was not definitely refused. The corps will proceed to-morrow to the Gare Saint-Lazare for entrainment. They will be sent, at first, to Rouen.

M.F.A. Granger, a young Frenchman, arrived to-day in Paris from New York, where he left his wife and family. He sailed on the *Rochambeau* with many of his countrymen, coming, like himself, to join the colors. M. Granger tells me that he saw near Lisieux a train of German prisoners, mostly cavalrymen, some of whom had been wounded by lance thrusts. They seemed resigned to their fate, without enthusiasm, and on the whole rather pleased at the prospect of being confined and fed in France, instead of remaining at the front. They said that they had no idea that England and Belgium were fighting against them, until they crossed swords with the Belgian cavalry, which they at first supposed were French.

Tuesday, August 25.

This is the twenty-third day of the war. Another warm, sunny day, with north-westerly breezes. Thermometer at five P.M. 24 degrees centigrade.

Better news from the front this morning. The great battle that has been raging for three days from Mons to Virton, during which the French and British attacks were repulsed, has been resumed, and renewed German attacks have been checked. Considerable anxiety as to the result nevertheless prevails. My concierge, Baptiste, for instance, shakes his head in a mournful way and says: "Ah! Monsieur, there is already terrible loss of life. My brother-in-law, who left Luxemburg three weeks ago to join his reserve regiment in France, is without a cent in the world, and what will become of his wife and two little children--the Lord only knows! Their little farmhouse, with all their belongings, has been burned, and nothing is left."

I breakfasted to-day at the restaurant Champeaux, Place de la Bourse. Two agents-de-change (official members of the Paris Stock Exchange) took very gloomy views of the situation. It seems, however, that the French rentes maintain their quotation of seventy-five francs. Mr. Elmer Roberts of the Associated Press and Mr. Hart O. Berg sat at our table. Both thought that the war would be much longer than at first expected and would depend upon how long Germany could exist, owing to the impossibility of obtaining food from abroad. "Eight months," said Mr. Berg.

After lunch I went with Roberts to see the departure of the first contingent of American volunteers from the Gare Saint-Lazare. These youths are a tall, stalwart lot, marching with a sort of cowboy swing. They were not in uniform, but wore flannel shirts, broad-brimmed felt hats, and khaki trousers. They carried a big American flag surmounted with a huge bouquet of roses, and alongside this a large French flag. They were loudly cheered as they were entrained for Rouen, where they will be drilled into effective shape.

I met Mrs. Edith Wharton, who remains in Paris, and is doing good work with her *ouvroir*, or sewing-circle, which, with Mrs. Thorne, she has organized in the Rue Vaneau. This *ouvroir* is to supply work to unmarried French women and widows. Among those who have liberally subscribed to this are Mrs. William Jay, Mrs. Elbert H. Gary, Mrs. Beach Grant, and Mrs. Griswold Gray.

I went in the afternoon to see Madame Waddington at her *ouvroir*, 156 Boulevard Haussmann. Madame Waddington makes an appeal by cable to the *New York Tribune*, calling upon all American women and men to aid her indigent French sewing-women, who are employed in making garments for the sick and wounded, for which they receive one and a half francs (thirty cents) and one meal, for a day's work. Madame Waddington wore a gray linen gown, with a red cross, and was working away very merrily, distributing materials to the women. She told me that her son had joined the colors as a sergeant in an infantry reservist regiment and was at the front.

M. Maurice Maeterlinck, the Belgian writer and philosopher, is living at his quaint Abbaye de Sainte-Wandrille, on the Seine near Caudebec. The author of *La Vie des Abeilles* has been helping the peasants gather the wheat harvest.

After three weeks, during which relief funds have been advanced to Americans at the Embassy, the demands for money continue to be as heavy as ever. Paris is a human clearing-house, into which new arrivals are now coming every day from Switzerland and elsewhere. Although many tourists have been helped and started on their way for the United States, new ones take their places before they are fairly out of the way.

Thus, although the Embassy hoped that it had succeeded in getting the persons in most urgent need off to America on the *Espagne*, the departure of that vessel has caused no let-up in the demand for funds, and some individuals who have already been helped once are now coming back for further assistance.

One of the negro song and dance artists, who was given some money a couple of weeks ago and who was supposed to have left on the *Espagne*, presented himself and asked for further funds after that vessel steamed. When asked how it happened that he did not go, as arranged, he replied: "'Deed, Ah overslept mahself."

"Considering that the boat train left at six o'clock in the evening," remarked Major Cosby, who has charge of the administration of the relief fund, "he would seem to be a good sleeper."

In the case of all persons who are helped, the stipulation is made that they must take the earliest possible means of transport to America. The Government has no intention of financing tourists who desire to visit Europe at this time. The sole object of the relief fund is to get them back to the United States as soon as possible.

In addition to the ordinary relief fund, one hundred and seventy thousand francs have been paid out at the Embassy this week by cable orders against funds already deposited with the Department of State. This is a purely business transaction, the Government having already received the full amount of the payment made, but it has been a source of much relief to many travelers.

Wednesday, August 26.

Twenty-fourth day of the war. Dull, cheerless weather, with a Scotch drizzle in the afternoon and heavy rain in the evening. Southwesterly wind. Temperature at five P.M. 20 degrees centigrade.

The great battle on the Sambre and Meuse continues with frightful slaughter on both sides. The allies have been partially forced back but resist with dogged determination.

Mrs. Hermann Duryea, a family relative of mine, and whose husband's horse "Durbar" won the English Derby this spring, has come to Paris for a few days from their country place near Argentan in Normandy, and is stopping at her apartment in the Avenue Gabriel. Mrs. Duryea's chauffeur, who is a young Frenchman, says that Belgian chauffeurs have reached Normandy from the north, telling harrowing tales of the brutality and cruelty of the Germans, and announcing that the "German cavalry and armored motor-cars would soon prevent people from leaving Paris." Mrs. Duryea, who is an exceedingly cool-headed, plucky woman, came to me for advice. I told her that there was no probability at present of communication from Paris to the westward being interfered with. She sent some of her servants home to the United States and made arrangements to rejoin her husband at Bazoches-en-Houlme, near Argentan. The chateau has, through the generosity of the Duryeas, been turned into a Red Cross hospital.

President Poincare has taken a leaf from Great Britain, and Premier Rene Viviani has reconstructed a new Cabinet with eminent men, representing all political parties, making a government of national defence. Since the outbreak of the war, the Cabinet has been taking advice from statesmen such as MM. Millerand, Delcasse, Briand, and Ribot. These men now form part of the Ministry, the formation of which was announced to a group of journalists at 11.30 this evening at the Ministry of War, when we assembled there for the usual nightly *communique*. The new

Cabinet is made up as follows: Prime Minister (without Portfolio), M. Rene Viviani; Vice-President of Council and Minister of Justice, M. Aristide Briand; Interior, M. Malvy; Foreign Affairs, M. Delcasse; War, M. Millerand; Navy, M. Augagneur; Finance, M. Ribot; Agriculture, M. Fernand David; Public Works, M. Marcel Sembat; Labor, M. Bienvenu-Martin; Commerce, M. Thomson; Public Instruction, M. Albert Sarraut; Colonies, M. G. Doumergue; Minister without Portfolio, M. Jules Guesde.

M. Etienne Alexandre Millerand is an illustrious member of the Paris Bar, who has been several times a cabinet minister. As head of the War Department, two years ago, he did more than any living Frenchman towards the reconstitution of true *esprit militaire* in the French army. He prepared the way for the three years' service, and reorganized the forces of the nation that had grown rusty during the decade that preceded the alarm caused by the German Emperor at Agadir. It is quite probable that M. Millerand will prove to be the Lazare Carnot--"The Organizer of Victory"--of the present war. With M. Theophile Delcasse as Minister of Foreign Affairs, French diplomacy cannot be in better hands. In calling upon M. Jules Guesde, socialist deputy for Lille, and upon M. Marcel Sembat, a red-hot socialist--both unified socialists and trusted friends of the late Jean Jaures, the Government is assured of the hearty support of the extreme "revolutionary" parties.

MM. Guesde and Sembat can certainly do the Government less harm *inside* the Cabinet than they might do *outside* of it. No better evidence that all bitterness of political parties is now in the melting-pot can be found than in the comment of the reactionary, ultra-Catholic, royalist *Gaulois*, which says: "We are to-day all united in the bonds of patriotism in face of the common enemy. We place absolute confidence in the men who have assumed a task, the success of which means the salvation of France and the triumph of civilization." M. Georges Clemenceau was offered a place in the Cabinet, but declined to accept it.

The appointment of General Joseph Simon Gallieni as commander of the army of Paris, and military governor, in succession to General Michel, means that France is resolved to put Paris in a thoroughly efficient state of defence, and to be ready for the worst possible emergencies. General Michel is an admirable organizer and administrator, but he has not had the vast military experience of General Gallieni, who is, by the way, a warm friend and comrade of the former military governor.

Moreover General Michel will now serve under General Gallieni's orders.

General Gallieni, as a strategist, enjoys the same high reputation as the commander-in-chief, General Joffre. He was born on April 24, 1849, at Saint-Beat in the department of the Haute Garonne. He entered the Saint-Cyr military academy in 1868, and was appointed a sub-lieutenant in the Third Regiment of Marine Infantry two years later, and he fought with his regiment through the war of 1870. Since then he has distinguished himself in Tonkin, Senegal, and Madagascar. Everywhere he has shown exceptional qualities, both as a soldier and administrator. His brilliant career finally led to his appointment as a member of the Higher Council of War, and, in acknowledgment of his great services, he was maintained on the active list after passing the age limit. He is a Grand Cross of the Legion of Honor.

President Poincare to-day confers further extraordinary powers upon General Joffre, authorizing him to exercise the almost sovereign right of promoting officers on the spot, just as Napoleon did, by simply naming them to the posts where he thinks they may be most useful. Thus, General Joffre can make a captain a colonel or a full-fledged general-of-division, by word of mouth. This privilege was not even granted by Napoleon to his marshals. These promotions are, however, only provisional during the war, and when peace is made, must be ratified by Parliament. This renders it possible to replace general officers, killed or wounded, by officers selected on the battlefield, and above all enables important commands to be filled by young officers, who give proof of their qualities in face of the enemy.

An idea of the infinite tragedy of war was brought home to many Parisians by a visit to the Cirque de Paris, where twenty-five hundred Belgian refugees, men, women, and children, have been provided with at least a temporary shelter.

The vast building, where so many famous boxing-matches have taken place, is now completely transformed. The ring has been cut in two, and hundreds of fauteuils have been placed in small groups so arranged as to form substitutes for beds. The boxes have been reserved for the many women with infants in arms.

Hardly were they installed, and hardly had the news spread in Paris of their miserable plight, than hundreds of Parisians visited the Cirque de Paris, all bringing gifts of food, drink, or clothing. It was a pathetic and at the same time a cheering sight to watch the refugees hungrily eating the midday meal which their French sympathizers had helped to provide. These refugees, many of whom carry babies in arms, will probably be sent into Normandy and Brittany to be cared for.

Thursday, August 27.

Twenty-fifth day of the war. Rain, severe thunderstorm at noon, northwest-erly wind. Temperature at five P.M. 17 degrees centigrade.

The huge German army, making its desperate struggle to invade France at many points from Maubeuge to the Vosges, is still held in check. Meanwhile the hand of fate, in the shape of the gigantic "Russian steam-roller," steadily advances in East Prussia. Cossacks have penetrated to within two hundred miles of Berlin.

Minister of War Millerand has revived the daily meetings of heads of depart-ments at the War Office. To-day the defensive condition of Paris was discussed. Work already in progress, under the supervision of General Gallieni, is pushed for-ward rapidly and methodically, and obstructions to artillery fire are being cleared away in the suburbs.

I rambled this morning through the so-called German quarter of Paris around the Rue d'Hauteville and between the main boulevards and the Rue Lafayette. All the German and Austrian *teutons* shops and places of business are closed. The *brasseries*, where the best Munich or Pilsener beer, with *wiener Schnitzel* or *leber-knoedel suppe* could be obtained until the end of July, are invisible behind signless iron shutters. The "intelligence section" of the German general staff had for years obtained precious military information through the enterprising, affable German commercial agents, restaurant keepers, commission merchants, waiters, and hotel errand boys (*chasseurs*) who thrived in this thrifty quarter.

A wounded sergeant of a Highland regiment, in talking yesterday with an American friend of mine at Amiens station, bitterly denounced the German prac-tice of concealing their advance by driving along in front of them numbers of refu-gee women and children. The Scottish sergeant said: "Our battalion was badly cut up. We were using our machine guns to repel a German advance. Suddenly we saw a lot of women and children coming along the road towards us. Our officers ordered us to cease firing. The refugees came pouring through our lines. Immediately be-hind them, however, were the German riflemen, who suddenly opened fire on us at short range with terrible effect. Had it not been for this dastardly trick of shov-ing women and children ahead of them at the points of their bayonets, we might have wiped out this German rifle battalion that attacked us, but instead of that, we were driven back. Damn these Germans!" With these words the Scottish sergeant, his right arm shattered from shoulder to elbow, climbed into the train of British wounded and was carried off towards Rouen.

A number of French wounded soldiers from the Northern Army arrived in Paris during the night and were sent to the Military Hospital, Rue des Recollets, to the Hospital of Saint-Louis, and to a hospital installed in the College Rollin. Among them were a number slightly wounded, but very few severely. Their spirit seems excellent, and all agree that few were killed considering the number of wounded.

All promise to obey orders more closely when they are well and back in the firing line, and not to be too rash. Rashness and too great anxiety to get at the foe seem, indeed, to have been the cause of a great many casualties.

Friday, August 28.

Twenty-sixth day of the war. Bright, clear weather with northeasterly breezes. Temperature at five P.M. 20 degrees centigrade.

I saw, in the Rue Franklin, M. Georges Clemenceau, the veteran demolisher of cabinets, and former Prime Minister, who in his youthful days was a mayor of the eighteenth arrondissement of Paris, the turbulent Montmartre quarter. M. Clemenceau severely criticizes the new Viviani Cabinet. "Viviani," said he, "asked me twice to form part of it. I declined because, in addition to personal reasons, the Ministry did not seem to me to realize the elements of power and action required by this war. Having this opinion, it would not be fair either to Viviani or to myself to enter into a combination where I should have to assume the responsibility for acts that to my mind would not adequately meet the emergency. Under the circumstances, there are only three ministers that count for anything; those of war, foreign affairs, and finance." M. Clemenceau said: "There must be something wrong with the mobilization scheme, because when our troops were outnumbered at the front, there were great quantities of young officers and men who for ten days had been awaiting, at their various points of assembly, orders to join their corps, and at the last moment were told to go home."

On the other hand, M. Millerand, Minister of War, has visited General Joffre at the army headquarters and returned to Paris to-night "very satisfied with the situation."

I took a spin in an automobile to-day to Versailles, and thence to Buc with its red brick aerodrome tower, sheds, and long rows of hangars. Here were groups of airmen in the rough, serviceable French sapper uniform--loose-fitting blue coat, blue trousers with a double red stripe, blue flannel scarf about their necks, as if they had all got sore throats, and blue pointed forage caps. Here is Chevillard, that wonderful gymnast of the air. There is Verrier, and here, driving a sporting-looking car, is Carpentier, whose more familiar costume is a pair of white slips and a pair of four-ounce gloves. For Carpentier has been mobilized, too. Instead of making thousands of dollars this month by his fight with Young Ahearn, and possibly other matches with Bombardier Wells and Gunboat Smith, he, too, is on the pay list of the army at next to nothing a day. He is attached to the flying center as a chauffeur, and that car he is driving is his own, only he cannot take it out without orders now.

Morning and evening they fly at Buc. They are constantly testing new machines, and then, when they have tested them, they fly off to the army on the eastern frontier, or to Amiens, perhaps. The other day a pilot even flew to Antwerp right across the German lines over the heads of the German army, but so high up that they never even guessed he was there. Then they practise bomb-dropping, too, and they are always on the alert for a possible Zeppelin raid on Paris. The other night a wireless message reached the Eiffel Tower from the frontier that one had started. It was midnight, and instantly the alarm was given at Buc. The airmen sleep in the hangars there, and in five minutes they had their machines wheeled out.

By the light of lanterns you could see mechanics running to and fro. The airmen themselves were hurriedly putting on helmets and woollen gloves and leather coats, for it is cold work hunting airships at midnight. Their little armory of bombs was quickly overhauled, and the belt of the machine gun that the man in the passenger's seat uses--the "syringe" as they call it--was filled, and the engines were set running to see that they were all right. But it was a false alarm after all, for, although a close lookout was kept everywhere between Paris and the frontier for the adventurous Zeppelin, and a hundred guns were craning up into the sky ready for her if she hove in sight, she never came, and the tired airmen turned in again to snatch a little sleep before morning parade.

Constantly airmen fly off to the front. Those who have been there say that the supply trains and the whole service is working splendidly. They have organized a new sport among the air-scouts. Every day, at the end of the day's reconnoitring, the airmen count the bullet-holes in the wings and body of their machines. The aeroplane that has the most is the cock machine of the squadrilla--six in the squadrilla--and holds the title until some one gets a bigger peppering and displaces him. They are very jealous of this distinction, and the counting has to be very carefully carried out by an impartial jury, for the cock aeroplane has the honor of carrying the mascot of the squadrilla.

Saturday, August 29.

Twenty-seventh day of the war. Sultry weather, with light northerly breezes. Temperature at five P.M. 26 degrees centigrade.

"Hold tight!" Such is the watchword given by the French Government, and French and British soldiers are holding tight for all they are worth against the slowly advancing German armies. Heavy fighting all along the lines from the Somme to the Vosges continues without a break. The Prussian Guard Corps and the Tenth German Army Corps have been driven back to Guise, in the department of the Aisne (one hundred and ninety kilometers from Paris), but on the French left the Germans have fought their way to La Fere (northwest of Laon, about one hundred and forty kilometers from Paris). In the eastern theater of the war, Koenigsberg has been invested by the Russians under Rennenkampf, who continue their advance towards Berlin.

Paris begins to realize that the war is coming closer to them, by the following official announcement:

DEFENCES OF PARIS

The Military Governor of Paris, in view of the urgent military requirements, has decided:

1. Within a delay of four full days, starting from August 30, all proprietors, occupants, and tenants of all descriptions of houses and buildings situated in the military zone of old and new forts must evacuate and demolish the aforesaid houses and buildings.

2. In the event of these instructions not being fulfilled within the prescribed

delay, these houses and buildings will be immediately demolished by military authority and the materials taken away.

The Military Governor of Paris, Commander of the Armies of Paris.

(Signed)

GALLIENI.

General Pau, the gallant one-armed general who commands the French Army of the East, arrived in Paris at four o'clock this afternoon, but the reason for his visit is naturally kept secret. He had a conference at the Ministry of War with M. Millerand. He called for a few moments at his residence in the Boulevard Raspail. General Pau's son, a sub-lieutenant of infantry, is lying wounded at the hospital at Troyes. General Pau had an informal conversation with President Poincare at the Elysee Palace, and leaves again for the front to-morrow morning.

Refugees from Belgium and northern France continue to pour into Paris. But the authorities, having had time to organize, are sending them on with very little delay to various places in the west and south of France.

It is impossible to prevent these frightened people from taking refuge in Paris, which they regard as a place of safety, and the only course open is to send them on as soon as possible.

Among the financial victims of the war are a number of Chinese students who have found their supplies of money from home suddenly cut off. A body of about sixty went to the Chinese Legation in the Rue de Babylone on Friday evening, and clamored for money.

The Minister, Mr. Liu Shih-shen, was out but, to the great disgust of the staff, the students invaded the dining-room and kitchen and commandeered the dinner which was being prepared for the Minister.

A message was sent to his Excellency, who dined at a restaurant. Meanwhile the students, having dined, began to gamble, and several made preparations to spend the night in the Legation. They were, however, expelled by the police.

At the meeting of the women's auxiliary of the American Ambulance at the Embassy this afternoon, many details in connection with the establishment and maintenance of the hospital in the Lycee Pasteur were discussed.

A committee was appointed for the special purpose of supplying with clothing such wounded soldiers as may be brought to the hospital.

It was announced that Miss Matthews will succeed Miss Cameron as the chairman of the sewing committee, the latter having been called to America by her brother's illness.

Mrs. W.K. Vanderbilt has offered to contribute many articles needed in the installation of the hospital, particularly such things as window curtains and other furnishings designed to make the institution as comfortable as possible for the sufferers.

For just four weeks now the American Government has been advancing money to citizens in need of it at the Embassy, and still the stream of applicants continues in about the same proportions as ever.

The undiminishing demand for funds is due largely to the fact that there are new arrivals in the city every day, but Major Cosby, who is in charge of the distribution of the money, believes that with the departure of the *Rochambeau* and the *Flandre* there will come a gradually lessening demand for assistance.

So far about five hundred persons have received money, and the total paid out for the four weeks is 62,100 francs. This represents about one hundred and twenty-five francs, or twenty-five dollars, apiece.

In addition to the Government fund, which is paid only to persons who accept it as a loan, about twenty-seven thousand francs, raised here in Paris, has been given outright to persons who for various reasons could not be assisted out of the Government fund.

Captain Brinton has also paid out from sixty to seventy thousand dollars to various persons upon cable orders from the Department of State in Washington. This represents a purely business transaction, as the money has first been deposited with the Government by friends in the United States. It has, however, been an exceedingly practical means of helping persons who otherwise might have had to fall back on the relief funds.

Sunday, August 30.

Twenty-eighth day of the war. Sunny, but sultry, August Sunday. Light northerly breeze, thermometer at five P.M. 26 degrees centigrade.

No let-up in the fighting. The Germans continue with wonderful tenacity their favorite tactics of rolling up their forces on their right, and then enveloping and striving to turn the Anglo-French left. The French left, as officially announced at the War Office, has been forced to yield ground. But the result of the gigantic battle in the department of the Aisne near La Fere, Guise, and Laon, on the road to Paris, still hangs in the balance.

It seems pretty certain that the French armies were concentrated too far to the east. The temptation to enter Alsace, where strong force is needless, was too great for the then war minister, M. Messimy, to withstand. France is paying for this now. For over twenty years it was an open secret among military authorities that the main German attack upon France would burst in through Belgium and the northern departments of France, which seem to have been left without adequate fortifications. Here is France's vulnerable point. For France to be now outnumbered in this theater of the war is strong evidence of her also being out-generaled. While the French have wasted needless troops in futile excursions beyond the Vosges and in the Ardennes, they seem to have been blind to the tremendous concentration of German fighting strength in the north. Had it not been for the solid, heroic resistance of the British army under Field-marshal Sir John French, on the extreme French left at Mons and Cambrai, it is very likely that the French would have sustained a crushing defeat. That the French should be outnumbered on the lines near La Fere seems incomprehensible and requires satisfactory explanation from the Ministry of War. Further proof of this primary fault is forthcoming in the proclamation issued to-day, calling to the colors the 1914 class, some two hundred and fifty thousand young men of twenty, due to join the army in October. Moreover, those classes of the reserves of the territorial army called up when the general mobilization order was issued and for some unaccountable reason ***actually sent home again***, have also been recalled.

In broad daylight, at 1.15 this afternoon, the Germans left their first visiting-card in Paris. This came in the shape of three bombs dropped from a German aeroplane, that made a curved flight over the city at an altitude of two thousand meters. The first bomb fell at the corner of the Rue des Vinaigriers and the Rue du Marais, another in the Rue des Recollets, and a third near an asylum for aged workmen on the Quai Valmy. The airman also let fall an oriflamme, two and a half meters long, bearing the black and white Prussian colors, ballasted by sand in an india-rubber football, attached to which was a letter, written in German, which ran as follows: "The German Army is at the gates of Paris. The only thing left for you to do is to surrender! (Signed) LIEUTENANT VON HEIDSSEN."

The first bomb wounded two women, one of whom died of her injuries at the hospital shortly afterwards. She was concierge of the house Number 39 Rue des Vinaigriers. No other damage was done. There were thousands of Parisians promenading the streets at the time. The news spread like wild-fire, but no panic, nor even undue excitement, ensued; the people of Paris are totally different to-day from what they were in 1870. Of course the intention of these aeroplane bomb-throwers, of whose exploits we shall probably hear a great deal, was to create a panic and demoralize the inhabitants, and especially to terrify women and children. This utterly failed. After dropping the three bombs and his *carte de visite*, the German aeroplane vanished towards the east. It seems strange that the flotillas of air-craft at Buc were thus caught napping and allowed the German air-lieutenant to escape.

I called in the afternoon upon Madame Waddington and her sister, Miss King. Madame Waddington was anxious about her grandchildren, who are at their country place not far from Laon, where the battle is now raging. Madame Waddington says that Mr. Herrick, whom she saw this morning, told her that if worse came to the worst, the seat of government would probably be transferred to Bordeaux.

A large sum in gold coin, it is said, has been taken from the vaults of the Bank of France and sent to Rennes. Sharp comment is elicited by an incident at the Travellers Club, a somewhat select resort of Americans, English, and other foreigners, in the former hotel of the famous beauty of the Second Empire, Madame de Paiva, in the Champs-Elysees. It appears that a wealthy and prominent German by birth, but naturalized American, Mr. X., casually remarked one day at the club that he did not intend to trouble himself to get a *permis de sejour* (permission to reside in Paris), because "when the German troops arrived in the capital, these papers would no longer be needed." Mr. X. was told that if he persisted in expressing such views, offensive to the members of the club and to the hospitable city in which the club was situated, his resignation would be forthwith accepted by the house committee. Mr. X. paid no attention to the warning, but when next he entered the club--a few days after the incident--he was informed that his name had been stricken from the list of members.

M. Adrien Mithouard, President of the Municipal Council, states that arrangements were made months ago to store a large quantity of flour in the city, so as to provide the civilian inhabitants with bread. This flour is in the hands of the military authorities, who have a considerably larger supply than was originally intended, and are still adding to it.

There will be no lack of coal. The army has accumulated enormous quantities, and the Gas Company has enough coal for five months. M. Mithouard also says he recently made a personal investigation of the water supply, and found that, even if the aqueducts were cut, the city would have two hundred and sixty thousand cubic meters of filtered water available every day from the Ivry and Saint-Maur waterworks; and even without these, Paris could still have two hundred and sixty thousand cubic meters a day chemically purified.

The Municipal Council has also approved a proposal to buy up certain provisions to be added to the necessaries of life for the civilian population.

M. Georges Clemenceau, the "parliamentary tiger," who, although remaining outside the Cabinet, is one of the greatest personal forces of France, has made a stirring statement to Mr. Somerville Story, editor of the **Daily Mail**. M. Clemenceau said:

"Yes, their guns are almost within sound of Paris. And what if they are? What if we were yet to be defeated again and again? We should still go on. Let them burn Paris if they can. Let them wipe it out, raze it to the level of the ground. We shall still fight on.

"This is not my personal resolve alone. The Government, too, is just as grimly determined. Do you know, it is strange that one should have been able to come to feel like this, but the Germans could destroy all these beautiful places that I love so much; they may blow up the museums, overthrow monuments--it would only leave me still determined to fight on.

"France may disappear, if you like. It may be called Frankreich, if you like. We may be driven back to the very Pyrenees. It will not abate one fraction our vigor and our decision.

"And in this terrible war we must all realize how unutterably great are the stakes. It is we in France and our friends in Belgium who are doomed to suffer the most bitterly. England will be spared much that we must endure. But we must all make sacrifices almost beyond reckoning. We are fighting for the dignity of humanity. We are fighting for the right of civilization to continue to exist. We are fighting so that nations may continue to live in Europe without being under the heel of another nation. It is a great cause; it is worthy of great sacrifices.

"I say this to convince you of the unbreakable spirit of the French nation.

"But the situation is not yet so grave. We knew our frontier would be invaded somewhere. We have many troops in reserve for the big battle that will follow this one.

"The Germans cannot besiege or invest Paris. Its size is too vast. Its defence will be assisted by the armies now fighting on the Oise, seventy miles away.

"The fortifications of Paris are by no means the feeble things they were in 1870. From the Eiffel Tower we can control the movements in co-operation with our armies in the provinces of France.

"The situation is in no way desperate, although the Germans have invaded France. France will fight on and on until this attempt to establish tyranny in Europe is overthrown."

Monday, August 31.

Twenty-ninth day of the war. Hot, somewhat hazy, summer weather, with faint northerly wind. Thermometer at five P.M. 27 degrees centigrade.

Kaiser William, who it appears was on the field during the battle of Charleroi, is pressing forward in hot haste, regardless of consequences, on the road to Paris, close behind the steel-tipped elite of his vast armies, consisting of the Royal Prussian Guard Corps and the famous Third Army Corps. To-morrow will be the anniversary of the Battle of Sedan. The "Mailed Fist" is doing his best to celebrate it by leading his legions to Paris. It is daredevil desperation that spurs him on, for nowhere, as yet, have the Franco-British armies been broken through, and they continue to present successive stone walls to the Teuton invasion, and oppose every inch of ground with dogged tenacity. The allied left wing has been forced--always by the traditional enveloping tactics on their right--to retreat, but they do so sullenly and in good order, making the Germans pay dearly for every step gained. The battle is raging continuously, and much depends upon which side first receives strong reenforcements to fill up the gaps made by tremendous losses. The Russian advance in East Prussia, according to accounts from Brussels, has already forced the Germans to send back to Berlin from their center at least one army corps.

There is hurry and skurry all day long among Parisians and foreign residents to get away from Paris to more peaceful towns in the south and west. The railway stations are so crowded that it is almost impossible, at the Gare of Saint-Lazare or at the Quai d'Orsay to get anywhere near the booking office. Motor-cabs are being hired at extravagant prices to convey families to Tours, Orleans, Le Mans, or Bordeaux. The bearing of the public however by no means resembles that of "nerves," and less still a panic.

I lunched to-day with Mr. Hulme Beaman, correspondent of the **London Standard**, and his charming wife, who live just across the way from me, in the Boulevard de Courcelles. Mr. Beaman passed Sunday at Poissy, where he usually goes fishing for gudgeon. At Acheres, the junction of the lines from Picardy and Belgium, he saw train after train filled with wounded French soldiers, who seemed in good spirits and who, in spite of their suffering, were burning to get back again to the front.

Another German air-lieutenant made a flight over Paris this afternoon and dropped two bombs near the Notre Dame Cathedral, but caused no damage; one of the projectiles fell into the Seine. The airman also tossed into Paris a German flag, to which was tied a postal card calling upon Paris to surrender. Groups watched the aeroplane, which never came lower than fifteen hundred meters, and women and children seemed rather amused at the sight.

A fugitive from Belgium, who was at Louvain shortly before the wilful destruction of the once beautiful university town, tells a curious story of a Dutchman who had a thrilling escape on the arrival of the Germans. He rushed for the Dutch flag, which, in his nervousness, he hoisted outside his door upside down. This then represented the French flag, and the Dutchman, who spoke no German, was immediately seized by the enemy and ordered to be shot. He was placed upright against a wall and was about to be riddled with bullets when his employer rushed up and told the Germans that they were going to shoot a Dutchman, which saved his life.

General Gallieni, Governor of Paris, has issued a decree prohibiting newspapers to publish "spread-head" lines extending over two columns in width. The news vendors are not allowed to shout out the news, or even the names of the papers on the streets. The type of headlines must not be of alarming size. In fact, a worldwide war was required to check the march of the sensational Paris "yellow" press.

The Minister of War has suppressed *sauf-conduits* for travelers leaving Paris by rail, but they must be provided with proper identification papers. The *laisser-passer*, delivered by the Prefecture of Police, is still required however for all who leave Paris by automobile.

The American committee, in a circular to Americans, signed by Judge Elbert H. Gary, chairman, and H. Herman Harjes, secretary, gives a warning against sensational reports about the "imminent occupation" of the city by the Germans, but expresses the opinion that "it would be wise for Americans who cannot be of special service during the war, or who are not required to remain by their business or professional interests, to leave the city in an orderly and quiet way, whenever reasonable opportunity is offered."

Tuesday, September 1.

Thirtieth day of the war, and forty-fourth anniversary of the Battle of Sedan. Oppressive sultry weather, with northeasterly wind. Thermometer at five P.M. 23 degrees centigrade.

The War Office *communique* to-night states that: "on our left wing, in consequence of the enveloping movement of the Germans and with the object of not entering into a decisive action under bad conditions, our troops have fallen back, some towards the south and others towards the southwest. The action which took place in the district of Rethel has enabled our forces to stop the enemy for the time being. In the center and on the right (Woevre, Lorraine, and the Vosges), there is no change in the situation."

This means that Emperor William is hacking his way still nearer to Paris. The failure however to realize his boast that he would celebrate the anniversary of Sedan by appearing within striking distance of the French capital may indicate that the turning point of this phase of the war is near at hand.

The allied troops north of Paris have established themselves in a fighting position more favorable than that into which an attempt was made to draw them. The dam still holds good, and breaches are being repaired.

The people of Paris are quite calm, in spite of false rumors and of pyrotechnics aloft executed by the German *taubes*.

At quarter past five this afternoon, I was walking across the Place de la Bourse to file a cable message to the **New York Tribune**. I heard a loud explosion, followed by clashing of broken glass. A projectile had fallen a hundred yards distant and hit the top of a house in the Rue de Hanovre. The *pompiers* were on the spot within three minutes, having been summoned by the fire-alarm box near the Bourse. No serious damage was done, but little lead pellets were found in profusion. When I heard the explosion, I looked up and saw an aeroplane at an altitude of about fourteen hundred meters vanishing towards the northeast. It was pale yellow, and white near the after part. It was a German *taube*. A sand-bag with a German Uhlan's pennant was dropped, bearing a card reminding Parisians that it was "the anniversary of Sedan, that they would soon be obliged to surrender the city, and that the Russians had been crushed on the Prussian frontier." Another bomb had been dropped on the roof of Number 29 Rue du Mail and broke into an empty room, but did not explode. A third bomb fell on a schoolhouse in the Rue Colbert; ricochetting off the wall, it fell into a courtyard, where it exploded and made a hole in the ground. Other bombs were dropped in the Rue de Londres and in the Rue de la Condamine; the last one injured a woman and a little girl, who were hit in the chest and head by fragments of the projectile. As the *taube* passed over the Pepiniere barracks, and the Place de l'Opera, at an altitude of perhaps twelve hundred meters, some soldiers fired at it with their rifles, but without effect. The German air-lieutenants have so far avoided the Eiffel Tower, where machine guns are placed.

The War Office announces that a flotilla of armored aeroplanes provided with machine guns has been organized to attack the German aeroplanes that fly over Paris. Spectacular sights are thus in store for us.

The American committee, constituted by the American Ambassador and including some of the most eminent Americans residing in Paris on the day of the declaration of war, has requested the Minister of War to supply it with formal proofs of the fact that the bombs which have fallen in Paris were thrown from a German aeroplane.

M. Millerand, in response to this request, has submitted to the American Ambassador and two delegates from the committee the complete "dossier."

The Ambassador, after having examined the evidence submitted to him, and to the members of the committee, decided to cable a report to his Government concerning these methods of warfare, which are not only acts against humanity, but, further, are in absolute violation of The Hague Convention, signed by Germany herself.

The committee has also decided to ask the American Government, while remaining loyal to its declaration of neutrality, to make a strong protest to the German Government.

The Minister of War has issued a decree calling up territorial reservists of all classes in the north and northeastern districts of France, not yet with the colors.

The French "left wing," which, as foreseen more than twenty years ago, must be the vulnerable spot in the defence of Paris, will very likely be forced to retire still nearer to the capital. In that case, a battle would be likely under the shelter of the Paris forts, which encircle the city at from thirty to forty kilometers from the Notre Dame. This belt of forts, connected by three lines of formidable entrenchments and rifle pits, now being dug, not only by the troops, but by thousands of Paris workmen out of regular employment, make a circumference of two hundred kilometers, or about one hundred and twenty-five miles. This line of defence would protect Paris and also a field army with all its own resources, and probably make it impossible for the Germans to completely invest the city, as they did in 1870. Meanwhile the allied armies outside of Paris would be able to keep the rest of the German armies "busy," and threaten the long line of German communications. Paris would thus be able to hold out for a long time. The Germans would obtain food supplies from the rich country that they occupy, but their supplies of ammunition, and of men to fill gaps in the fighting units of the first line, must become precarious. Meanwhile the Russian "steam-roller" is moving towards Berlin.

At six o'clock this evening the following decree was issued by the Prefecture of Police:

"By order of the Military Governor of Paris, no civilian automobile carriage will be allowed to leave Paris from today. This order has been immediately enforced."

Streams of people from the regions to the north of Paris within the sphere of the German operations are swarming into Paris, bringing their belongings with them. I saw a train pull slowly into the Gare du Nord laden with about fifteen hundred peasants--old men, women, children--encumbered with bags, boxes, bundles, fowls, and provisions of various kinds. The station is strewn with straw, on which country folk fleeing from the Germans are soundly sleeping for the first time in many days. These refugees are being shunted on to the ***chemin de fer de la ceinture*** and proceed around the city to other stations, from which they are transported towards the south.

Tens of thousands of Parisians throng the railway stations, seeking their turn to buy tickets to points outside the city. At the Gare de Lyon, Montparnasse, d'Orsay, d'Orleans, people are standing in lines ten abreast and a quarter of a mile in length, waiting for hours and hours to book for Bordeaux, Biarritz, Brest, Rennes, or Nantes. Some of these people have waited from seven in the morning until three in the afternoon to obtain tickets.

If matters get worse, President Poincare and the Ministry will establish themselves at Bordeaux. Ambassador Herrick intends to remain in Paris, as Minister Elihu Washburne did in 1870. He will delegate a secretary to represent the United States Embassy at the seat of government. Perhaps Mr. Sharp, the newly appointed Ambassador, might be utilized for this purpose.

A convoy of one hundred and forty British soldiers, wounded in the recent fighting in the Aisne Department, arrived at nine o'clock this morning at the Gare du Nord.

Most of them were shot in the legs and arms, but in spite of their sufferings, none of them showed the least sign of being broken in spirit. As they were transported from the train, there were touching demonstrations of sympathy from the crowd, which the wounded men acknowledged to the best of their ability.

By a pretty little attention on the part of the Red Cross workers in Chantilly, all the men wore a flower and had been the recipients of refreshments and fair words of encouragement.

There was quite a procession of wounded of various nationalities at the station, and scenes were witnessed which caused the tears to start in many eyes. A group of Belgian soldiers, including several wounded, encountered the British convoy on their arrival, and hearty handshakes were exchanged.

Half an hour after the arrival of the British wounded, a party of thirty Turcos wounded in the battle of Guise came in and were in turn accorded an ovation. According to one of the men, they fought for nine days and nights without a break, but were gratified in the end by beating back the enemy. With one voice they declared that they are impatient to get back again into the fighting line.

A British private, wounded in the leg by a German shell, described the fighting around Mons on Sunday week as "terrific." They first got the German shell fire quite unexpectedly near the railway station. Two of their battalions marched through the streets of Mons and were fired on from house windows by the Germans. Some of the German shells, he said, were filled with broken glass and emitted a suffocating gas when they exploded.

Mr. Elbert H. Gary, chairman of the American Committee, left to-day by automobile for Havre, whence he expects to start for New York on Saturday on the *France*. It was decided at the meeting of the committee yesterday afternoon that Mr. Gary should, though absent, retain the chairmanship, with Mr. H. Herman Harjes, the secretary, acting as presiding officer. Mr. Lazo, the assistant secretary, becomes secretary in Mr. Harjes' place.

Mr. F. E. Drake, Major Clyde M. Hunt, Mr. Henry S. Downe and Mr. W. H. Ingram were added to the membership of the committee.

Wednesday, September 2.

Thirty-first day of the war. Beautifully clear weather, cloudless sky, northeast-erly wind. Temperature at five P.M. 25 degrees centigrade.

German prisoners declare that Emperor William has made it known to every soldier that his orders are to "take Paris or die." A German cavalry division came into contact with British troops yesterday in the forest of Compiegne. The British captured ten field guns. But the right wing of the German army, which ever since the battles of Charleroi and Mons has enveloped and turned the allied left, con-tinues its advance. The allied troops have retired partly to the south and partly to the southwest. A great battle must consequently take place within the range of the Paris forts. Work on the entrenched lines connecting the forts is actively carried out and is said to give every satisfaction. The positions, believed to be impregnable, are strengthened by ingenious arrangements of barbed wire. It is reported that some of this barbed entanglement contains live wires fed by the electric batteries of the defence.

In a stirring editorial in his newspaper ***L'Homme Libre***, M. Georges Clemenceau frankly faces the situation now that "the Germans are close to Paris." He adds: "We have left open the approach to Paris, while reserving to ourselves flank attacks on the enemy. If the forts do their duty, this move may be a happy one. From what we have seen of him, General Joffre belongs to the temporizing school. At this moment there are no better tactics. The supreme art will be to seize the instant when temporization must give way to a carefully prepared offensive movement. I have full confidence in General Joffre."

Lord Kitchener made a rapid incognito visit to Paris yesterday, where he met Field-marshal Sir John French. As far as can be ascertained, Lord Kitchener went to the front and had a conference with General Joffre. There seems to be no doubt but what General Joffre's plans have the heartiest approval and support of Lord Kitchener. French troops from the eastern theater of the war are being brought up rapidly, so as to attack the German lines of communications, possibly near Rethel. Reenforcements are coming in rapidly from England, and a large new army has formed, at Le Mans, and will soon be ready to take the field with great effect.

The usual six o'clock serenade of the German air-lieutenants this afternoon drew forth a few rifle shots from roofs of Paris houses, and even a quick-firing gun was discharged at one of these ***taubes***. But the distance was too great, and the two German aeroplanes vanished shortly before seven in a northerly direction.

This evening President Poincare and the French Government removed the seat of government from Paris to Bordeaux, and the following proclamation was issued:

Frenchmen,

For several weeks, during desperate fighting, our heroic troops have struggled with the enemy's army. Our soldiers' valiance has brought them marked advantages on several points. But to the north the advance of the German forces has compelled us to draw back.

This situation imposes on the President of the Republic and the Government a painful decision. To safeguard the national salvation, the public powers have as a duty momentarily to leave the city of Paris.

Under the command of an eminent leader, a French army, full of courage and zest, will defend the capital and its patriotic population against the invader. But the war must be pursued at the same time over the rest of the land.

Without peace or truce, without halt or faltering, the sacred struggle for the honor of the nation and the reparation of violated right will be continued.

None of our armies is cut into. If some of them have undergone losses--too great losses--the vacant places have been immediately filled by the depots, and the call of the recruits ensures for us for to-morrow further resources of men and energies.

Fight and stand firm--such must be the watchword of the allied armies, British, Russian, Belgian, and French.

Fight and stand firm; while on the sea the British help us to cut our enemy's line of communications with the outside world.

Fight and stand firm; while the Russians continue to advance to strike the decisive blow in the heart of the German Empire.

It is the duty of the Government of the Republic to direct this stubborn resistance.

Frenchmen will rise on every side for the sake of independence. But in order that this formidable struggle shall be conducted as efficaciously and with as much spirit as possible, it is essential that the Government should be left free to act.

At the request of the military authorities, therefore, the Government will be temporarily transferred to a point in French territory where it can remain in constant relations with the whole of the country.

The Government requests members of Parliament not to remain too distant from it, in order that, in conjunction with them and with their colleagues, they may be able to form a solid core of national unity in the face of the enemy.

The Government leaves Paris only after having assured, by every means within its power, the defence of the city and the entrenched camp.

It knows that there is no necessity to recommend the admirable population of Paris to remain calm, resolute, and self-possessed. Every day the people show that it is equal to this highest duty.

Frenchmen,

Let us be worthy of these tragic circumstances. We shall win the victory finally.

We shall win it by untiring will, endurance, and tenacity.

A nation which is determined not to perish, and which recoils neither before suffering nor sacrifice, is sure to conquer.

*   *   *   *   *

This proclamation had a good effect on the population.

The wife of my concierge voiced the popular sentiment when she said this evening: "Ah! Monsieur! We may have some pretty bad *quarts d'heures* here, but we have such confidence that all must end well, that my husband's old mother and our little children will remain in Paris with us." This remark was made five minutes after a German air-lieutenant had flown over the roof of the houses in my street, Rue Theodule-Ribot, and had dropped near the Parc Monceau a bomb that made a terrific noise, but did no damage.

Thursday, September 3.

Thirty-second day of the war. Dazzling sunshine, cloudless sky, and light northeasterly wind. Thermometer at five P.M. 27 degrees centigrade.

The forward movement of the Germans, the "Paris or Death" rush of the Kaiser, seems, for a moment at least, to have come to a standstill. Although precautions had been taken in expectation of a German attack from the region of Compiegne-Senlis, no contact, says the French official *communique*, occurred to-day. In the northeast all is reported quiet.

Disappointed Parisians scanned the sky in vain for their five o'clock *taube*. A *marchand-de-vin* on the famous "Butte" of Montmartre arranged a tribune with numbered seats commanding a splendid view of the city. Field-glasses were on hand for hire. Orchestra stalls were paid for at the rate of ten cents a seat. The performance was announced to begin at half-past five. This worked very well yesterday, when the evolutions of the two German air-lieutenants, accompanied by pyrotechnic display, netted a lucrative harvest. To-day, however, the enterprising theatrical manager was forced by his public to return the money at the "box office;" this was promptly done, the performance "being postponed." The postponement was due to the appearance of several French aeroplanes, which evidently had been sighted by the Germans.

Now that the French Government has gone to Bordeaux and temporarily transferred the capital to Gascony, the only heads of the diplomatic corps remaining in Paris are the American Ambassador; the Spanish Ambassador, the Marquis de Villa Urrutia; the Swiss Minister, M. C. Lardy; the Danish Minister, M. H.A. Bernhoft; and the Norwegian Minister, Baron de Wedel Jarlsberg.

That American property may be safeguarded, in the extremely improbable event of an occupation of the city by the Germans, Ambassador Herrick requests all American citizens owning or leasing houses or apartments in the city of Paris or its vicinity to register their names, with descriptions of their dwellings, at the Embassy. If worse comes to the worst, notices will be posted on American dwellings, giving them the protection of the American flag.

Mr. Robert Bacon, former Ambassador to France, is stopping at the Hotel de Crillon in the Place Vendome. He lunched to-day with Mr. Herrick, and both express optimistic views of the situation from military, diplomatic, and financial standpoints.

My servant, Felicien, telephoned me from Aubervillier, some ten kilometers from Paris, saying that he, together with four men of his squadron, had become separated from his regiment, the Thirty-second Dragoons. They had lost their horses in the marshes and woods near Chantilly during a cavalry engagement and had been instructed to make their way to Paris and rejoin their regimental depot at Versailles. The party was in charge of their sergeant, who explained that the regiment had at first been sent towards Metz, where they took part in the daily fighting all along the line there, and that suddenly they were entrained and rushed across country to Peronne, to check the advance of the Germans in their march upon Paris. This seems to indicate that the French generals did not fully appreciate until too late the really vital importance of the concentrated rush upon Paris of the right wing of the German armies, where all their strength had been assembled. The dragoons seemed pretty worn out, but were in good spirits and anxious to get back again in the fighting line. But they must go to Versailles to obtain their remounts. Sophie made a succulent lunch for them in the kitchen. They ate beefsteak, potatoes, cabbage, fruit, rice, and cheese, washed down with half a dozen bottles of light claret.

Every one seems to be trying to get away from Paris. It is a sort of exodus. I watched my opposite neighbors, Baron and Baroness Pierre de Bourgoing--the lat-ter better known as Suzanne Reichenberg of the Comedie Francaise--getting into their motor-car at half-past five this morning, accompanied by a maid and a pet dog. Baron de Bourgoing was in the uniform of a captain of territorials. He will go with his wife as far as the outer fortifications in the direction of Versailles.

The news of the election of Cardinal Jacques della Chiesa as Pope, with the title Benoit XV, does not arouse as much public interest here as does the nomination of M. Emile Laurent as Prefect of Police, in place of M. Hennion who, on account of ill health, retires at his own request. M. Laurent has for twenty-three years been secretary-general of the Prefecture of Police. He was born in 1852. He is thoroughly familiar with every phase of Paris life. He is a man of great energy and of prompt decision. He is a very kind-hearted man and has done much toward relieving mis-ery in the capital. The appointment is a very popular one and gives general satisfac-tion.

Friday, September 4.

Thirty-third day of the war. Hot, sultry day with light northeast wind. Thun-derstorm, with heavy rain in the evening. Temperature at five P.M. 28 degrees centigrade.

Americans still left in Paris were very busy to-day registering their addresses at the chancellery of the Embassy in the Rue de Chaillot. They had to have their leases with them. I registered for my little place at Vernon and also for my apartment in the Rue Theodule-Ribot. Among well known Americans whom I saw at the chan-cellery were Messrs. James Gordon Bennett, De Courcey Forbes, Julius and Robert Stewart, William Morton Fullerton, Mrs. Duer, formerly Mrs. Clarence Mackay, Dr. Joseph Blake, and about a hundred others. All sorts of wild rumors about the approaching Germans were current. One tremulous little lady said that "when the Germans entered the forest of Compiegne, the French set fire to the woods, and then shot down the Germans like rabbits as they fled from the burning thicket!"

I met here Mr. Robert Dunn, war correspondent of the **New York Evening Post**, who is the only newspaper man I have talked with who really saw the fight-ing near La Cateau and Saint Quentin. Mr. Dunn went on a train with his bicycle last week, provided only with a **laisser-passer** for Aulnay in the Department of the North. The train was brought to a stop near Aulnay, and the passengers were informed that German cavalry occupied the line a couple of kilometers further on. Every one got out. Mr. Dunn jumped on his bicycle and wheeled off to La Cateau. Here he met the British retreating in good order. He remained with them as they retired toward Saint Quentin. He saw them spread out in thin lines and pick off the German gunners by their splendid marksmanship. Most of the British were wounded by shells. Very few of them had bullet wounds. At Saint Quentin a few Highlanders came limping along, thoroughly exhausted with their five days' continuous fighting. But although pale and hungry, their jaws were set with determined grit. Their superb pluck impressed Mr. Dunn immensely. As they were sitting at a cafe, some French soldiers led away a German spy, with a towel wrapped around his eyes. The man was executed.

I met a British staff officer at Brentano's bookstore, as he was buying maps of the environs of Paris. I told him that Lord Kitchener had been to Paris and had conferred with M. Millerand, the French Minister of War. The officer said: "I am glad to hear of *that*, because at a certain phase of the fighting in the north, the *French completely failed to support us*."

I called upon Mr. William G. Sharp, the newly appointed United States Ambassador, and upon Mr. Robert Bacon, the former United States Ambassador. Both are stopping at the Hotel de Crillon. The Paris newspapers seem highly pleased at this "strong diplomatic manifestation"--the American Ambassador of yesterday, the American Ambassador of today, and the American Ambassador of tomorrow --constituting a delegation from the United States to see that the rights of universal humanity are respected. Parisians salute the Star Spangled Banner as it floats over the American Embassy as the symbol of the "World's Vigilance against Barbarity,"--such are the words of *La Liberte*. M. Gabriel Hanotaux, writing in the *Figaro*, attaches equal importance to the attitude of the United States as interpreted by its three representatives, saying: "Mr. Herrick is very happily not leaving us. He has followed the whole course of events which led to this fatal war, watching with a just and noble spirit. He has kept his Government accurately informed of all, and he will continue at the head of the Embassy."

The *Matin* says, "that of all the diplomatists accredited to France, it was Mr. Herrick who took the gallant initiative to remain in Paris, and Parisians deeply appreciate this. In making this choice, Mr. Herrick said that he regarded Paris not only as the capital of France, but as that 'Metropolis of the World' spoken of by Marcus Aurelius. He feels that he is the American Ambassador to both these cities. In his eyes this 'Metropolis of the World' possesses a Government, invisible doubtless, but perpetually present, and one with which he wishes to remain in touch. It is at one and the same time to Paris, in its period of trial, and to the fatherland of the human race, that Mr. Herrick wishes to give the pledge of his affection. Thus he is remaining as a link between those of his compatriots who are residing among us and the citizens of the free Republic across the sea that has more than once declared itself the sister Republic and which professes as much love for our 'traditions' as we ourselves esteem the passion for 'progress', of which it gives the example."

Saturday, September 5.

Thirty-fourth day of the war. Hazy autumnal morning, clear and hot in the afternoon, with light northerly breeze. Thermometer at five P.M. 26 degrees centigrade.

Germans appear to have evacuated the Compiegne-Senlis region, and are apparently moving towards the southeast, thus continuing a movement that began on Friday. General Cherfils, the military critic of the **Gaulois**, taking a very optimistic view of the situation, thinks the movement may be to assure a retreat by some route other than by a return through Belgium. General Cherfils says: "This rush of the German right wing upon Paris is the last bluff of terrorism of the last German Emperor! The Kaiser thought that he could frighten us and induce France to make peace. After which he would be free to return with his armies against Russia."

Mr. d'Arcy Morel, the financial correspondent of the **London Daily Telegraph**, came to see me to-day. He lives at Reuil, in the military zone northwest of Fort Mount-Valerian. He had been up all night, getting his belongings to Paris, and had just sent his little daughter to Dieppe on her way to England. Mr. Morel said that the night trains out of Paris at the Gare Saint-Lazare were filled to overflowing. No lights were permitted in the cars, and a dozen soldiers with loaded rifles were placed in a car just behind the locomotive, and a dozen more soldiers at the rear end of the train. These trains stop at every station and take about ten hours to reach Dieppe, instead of four hours as usual. Precautions of guarding the trains are made because several German armored motor-cars had been signalled dashing about near Marly and Pontoise. The gardener of my little place at Vernon, which is on the western line of the Seine, at a point where it is intersected by a strategic line between Chartres in the south and Gisors and Beauvais in the north, seems to be confident that Vernon will not be occupied by the Germans, for he managed to send me today a big basket full of peaches, pears, string beans, and green corn.

To-day the first oysters make their appearance! This event, trivial in itself, is significant as showing that the Paris central markets are able to supply Parisians not only with necessities but with luxuries. The mute oyster that comes in with the months having the letter "R" in their names bears eloquent testimony to uninterrupted communications.

I looked in for a few moments this afternoon at the National Library in the Rue de Richelieu. No signs of war here! A score of inveterate bookworms were pondering over dusty volumes, inquisitive writers were exploring literature bearing upon the war of 1870, seeking precedents and parallels for coming events; a few ladies were looking up files of old newspapers and fashion plates. The National Library seemed exactly as in the most peaceful days.

I lunched to-day at the restaurant Beauge, in the Rue Saint-Marc, a favorite resort of journalists. The manager told me that it would be closed that evening. It seems that he had received a "third warning" not to keep open after half-past nine. As he could never pluck up courage to eject his customers while enjoying succulent repasts, he decided to shut up his place altogether. The suggestion made by an Irishman, Mr. Sullivan of Reuter's Agency, to employ a London "chucker-out" did not at all appeal to his notions of the traditions of Parisian gastronomic hospitality.

I met to-day another British officer buying books at Brentano's. He gave me a picturesque description of the German method of advance. "It is the scientific development of the wild, fanatic, life-regardless, condensed rush of the Soudan dervishes," he said. "The Germans mass together all their big field guns. They close in around them serried infantry, goaded on by their wonderful, machine-made, non-commissioned officers, who prick them with sword bayonets, and whenever, from wounds or from sheer exhaustion, men fall out, they are shoved aside, to die by the roadside, or to be trampled under foot, like mechanical tools that have become useless. The German officers and non-commissioned officers are utterly regardless of life. The German flanks are protected by quantities of machine guns placed so close together that their gunners jostle one another. This strange engine of modern warfare creeps on like a monster of the apocalypse, carrying all before it. Aeroplanes hovering over the fronts of the columns direct movements by signalling. The dense, serried mass of infantry offers a splendid target. The losses must have been frightful--exceeding anything recorded in modern war. The German infantry are poor marksmen. They don't know how to shoot. Scarcely any of our men were wounded by bullets. Nearly all the wounds were inflicted by shells."

The Marquis de Valtierra has been appointed Spanish Ambassador to the French Republic, in place of the Marquis de Villa Urrutia, who has resigned. The new Ambassador, who has presented his credentials to President Poincare at Bordeaux, and who is expected to arrive in Paris to-morrow, has not followed a diplomatic career. He is a captain-general --a title corresponding with that of an army corps commander in France--and until a few days ago was in command of the military region of Burgos.

News that the representatives of France, Great Britain, and Russia have signed an agreement in London not to make peace without previous understanding with the others, meets with popular approval here, and is taken as further evidence that the allies are determined to fight the war to a finish.

Sunday, September 6.

Thirty-fifth day of the war. Ideal September weather, with light easterly wind. Temperature at five P.M. 24 degrees centigrade. The moon is now full.

Instead of making a ferocious **attaque brusquee** on Paris, the four army corps composing the German right wing are moving southeastward, in a supreme effort to crush the left flank of the French center, which is reported to be engaged with the main German forces near Rethel, striving to cut off and surround the French center, and thus achieve a second, but far more gigantic, Sedan. In any event, the Germans are certainly moving away from Paris to the southeast.

Paris assumes a holiday aspect. Thousands of people made excursions to the suburbs of the city, and particularly to the Bois de Boulogne, to see something of the preparations for the defence. Boys and girls from boarding-schools, under care of their teachers, were among those who watched gangs of men digging wide and deep trenches, while trees that obstructed the ground in the vicinity were being cut down.

The daily crop of Paris newspapers is becoming beautifully less. The *Temps* published its last Paris issue on Friday and has transferred its headquarters to Bordeaux. M. Georges Clemenceau's *Homme Libre* has ceased to appear. So also have the *Gil Blas* and *Autorite*. The *Daily Mail* has migrated to Bordeaux. Most of the newspapers that remain are published on a single sheet. The veteran *Journal des Debats* announces that for one hundred and twenty-five years it has appeared in Paris, being interrupted only at rare and brief intervals when provisional governments, resulting from violence, by brute force prevented publication. *Le Journal des Debats* will continue to be printed and published in Paris "so long as it is materially possible to do so." M. Arthur Meyer, editor and proprietor of *Le Gaulois*, announces that he will "remain in Paris in 1914 as he did in 1870." He will continue to edit and publish the *Gaulois* in Paris, having around him "a small family of editors and reporters, who replace my own family, now, Alas! far away!" The *Echo de Paris* continues to publish each day an edition of four pages. So also does *Le Figaro*. The *Matin* and *Liberte* appear on single sheets.

The European edition of the *New York Herald* appears every day on its nice white glazed *papier de luxe*, in a four-page edition Sundays, and on a single sheet on week days. The *Paris Herald*, as it is familiarly called, is printed half in English and half in French. The war has not frightened away the venerable "Old Philadelphia Lady," who daily continues, as she has done since Christmas eve, 1899, to put the following question:

TO THE EDITOR OF THE HERALD:--
I am anxious to find out the way to figure the temperature from Centigrade to Fahrenheit and vice-versa. In other words, I want to know, whenever I see the temperature designated on Centigrade thermometer, how to find out what it would be on Fahrenheit's thermometer.

OLD PHILADELPHIA LADY.
Paris, December 24, 1899.

Monday, September 7.

Thirty-sixth day of the war. Hot September weather, with brisk east wind. Temperature at five P.M. 24 degrees centigrade.

The great battle begun Sunday morning continues with slight advantages obtained by the allies and extends over a front of one hundred and thirty miles, from Nanteuil le Haudoin, on the allied left, to Verdun. The allies occupy very strong positions. Their left is supported by Paris, their right by the fortresses of Verdun, and their center by the entrenched camps of Mailly, just south of Vitry-le-Francois.

About thirty American and English newspaper men met at lunch to-day at the restaurant Hubin, Number 22 Rue Brouot. Among those present were Fullerton, Grundy, MacAlpin, Williams, Knox, Reeves, O'Niel, Sims, and others. Every one was in fine spirits, the trend of feeling being that Paris was the most interesting place to be in just now, and that perhaps the best story of the war may yet be written in Paris.

I drove in a cab with MacAlpin to the Gare du Nord to meet a train of British wounded that was expected to arrive there. We found the station almost deserted. A reserve captain of the Forty-sixth Infantry, whose left forearm had been smashed by a shell, arrived and was very glad to get some hot soup provided by the railroad ambulance women. Saw a brigadier-general and his staff going full speed in a motor-car to the east. Artillery firing was heard this morning to the east of Paris, but was no longer audible after eleven A.M. While sitting at a cafe opposite the Gare du Nord, I noticed the huge statues of "Berlin" and "Vienna" over the front of the building, and wondered if they would remain intact during the war. Driving to the Gare de l'Est, we saw gangs of workmen with entrenching tools, going into trains, under the direction of engineer officers, to dig rifle pits.

The sanitary condition of Paris is excellent. No epidemic of any kind is reported. There were several cases of scarlatina, but the number is insignificant.

The board of governors of the American Hospital has turned over its responsibility to the American Ambulance Committee, which will manage the Hospital service for the benefit of the French army, at the Lycee Pasteur, Neuilly. The committee is composed of William S. Dalliba, honorary chairman, Reverend Doctor S.N. Watson, chairman, Messrs. Laurence B. Benet, Charles Carroll, F.W. Monahan, and I.V. Twyeffort.

I met in the Rue de la Paix two Irish cavalry soldiers, who had become detached from their squadron during the operations north of Paris. "The last place we remember fighting at was **Copenhagen**," said one of the men. But on being further questioned, it turned out that Copenhagen was Tipperary dialect for Compiegne.

The **Herald** has decided to remain in Paris, but its price will be twenty-five centimes instead of fifteen centimes. The reasons for the increased price are that advertisements, the main source of revenue for a newspaper, have almost completely disappeared. The **Herald** at present is being run at a loss of thirty-five thousand francs a week. As the editor points out: "This may be journalism, but it is not business." The increased price will probably diminish the weekly loss.

Tuesday, September 8.

Thirty-seventh day of the war. Cloudy weather with rain in the afternoon. Brisk southeasterly wind. Thermometer at five P.M. 22 degrees centigrade.

The allied armies are more than holding their own on the vast line between the Ourcq and Verdun. Meanwhile all precautions are being taken by the Military Government of Paris for an eventual siege. The Bois de Boulogne resembles a cattle ranch. The census of the civil population of the "entrenched camp of Paris," just taken with a view of providing rations during a possible siege, shows that there are 887,267 families residing in Paris, representing a total of 2,106,786 individuals of all ages and both sexes. This is a decrease of thirty percent since the last census in 1911. The health of the city is excellent. The census sheets notify inhabitants that gas during a siege must be used exclusively for lighting purposes and never for cooking or heating. This will cause some tribulation in the small menages, where the cheap, popular, and handy gas-stove has replaced the coal or charcoal ovens and ranges.

The ram came on this afternoon at four, while a large crowd of Parisians stood in the square in front of the church of Saint-Etienne du Mont, beside the Pantheon, but it failed to disperse the faithful, who were taking part in the outdoor service of homage to Sainte-Genevieve, the protectress of Paris, whose remains are buried in this small church of the Gothic-Renaissance period (1517-1620), one of the most beautiful of all the sacred edifices of France.

Those who recently hastened away from Paris in search of a place of refuge, quiet, and safety, have met with many disappointments. The roads to Tours are blocked with vehicles of every description, many of them filled with refugees who have turned them into temporary dwellings. Automobiles are brought to a standstill for lack of benzol. Everything on the way from Paris to Bordeaux is requisitioned. At Orleans, people wander about vainly seeking a place in which to sleep. The town is filled. People buy ham and sausages, which they eat in cafes or in the streets. At Blois, the citizens offer to lodge refugees and travelers at the rate of five francs a day. The Blois people are very hospitable and do not seek to unduly profit by the situation. The Grand Hotel is of course overflowing, but the prices remain the same as in ordinary times. At Tours, the inhabitants are less hospitable and more avaricious. One of the biggest hotels in the town asks fifty francs (ten dollars) for a simple armchair in which to pass the night. Three special trains yesterday carried away to Provence the inmates of the insane asylums of Bicetre and Charenton. It was a weird sight to see these men and women, utterly unconscious of the war, gazing with nervous uncertainty upon the strange scenes through which they were conducted to the Orleans Station, somewhat like helpless flocks of sheep.

Shortly after leaving the large room at Number 31 Boulevard des Invalides, where the official *communiques* are now given out to the French and foreign press, I met a sergeant of an infantry regiment who had been wounded during the fighting between Coulommier and Ferte-Gaucher. "At daybreak on Sunday," he said, "we were sent forward to prevent the German infantry from making their favorite turning movement on our left wing. Our orders were to hold on to the enemy and prevent his advance until the allied troops near Meaux had repulsed the German attack being made in their direction. Early in the afternoon, the Germans retired from Meaux before the allied divisions. We advanced and drove them north of Ferte-Gaucher. The fighting lasted all night and became very severe on Monday morning, but shortly afterwards the Germans offered but slight resistance. For thirty kilometers we followed up two German infantry regiments, supported by their cavalry and a section of artillery. During their retreat, the Germans did not fire a single shot. We soon succeeded in cutting off a detachment of infantry and in capturing seven field guns and two machine guns. One of the prisoners, an infantry sergeant, admitted that his men were short of ammunition, and that their orders were to use as little of it as possible. It was during the last combat that I was wounded in the thigh by a Prussian officer, who cut me with his sword as I was trying to disarm him."

A wounded French infantry lieutenant says that the German troops seem "fatigued and fagged out." Another officer says that in the trenches near Coulommier, a dozen German infantry soldiers were found dead, having been killed by French .75 millimeter shells, and were in the same attitudes of firing that they had taken at the moment when they had been "crisped" by death. An Algerian Turco was found dead, grasping his rifle, the bayonet of which had pierced and killed a German soldier. Both were corpses, but stood in grim death like a group of statuary.

I received to-day a letter from my gardener at Vernon. He says that the roads are filled with refugees, who are being sent on to Brittany by way of Louviers. Motorists along the roads say that they have passed continuous lines of refugees, sometimes seventy kilometers in length. The Chateau de Bizy is transformed into a hospital and so also is the Chateau des Penitents at Vernonnet. Most of the injured have slight wounds in the arms or legs. Many of them, after five days' treatment, are able to go back to the front.

Wednesday, September 9.
Thirty-eighth day of the war. Somewhat cooler weather, with cloudy sky and with south to southwesterly wind, at times blowing in sharp gusts. Thermometer at five P.M. 21 degrees centigrade.

The air is still overcharged with uncertainty as to the result of the great battle along the front of one hundred and twenty miles between the Ourcq and Verdun. Will the Germans succeed in forcing their tremendous wedge through the French center near Vitry and separate the allied armies to the west and around Paris, from the great French armies to the east and around Verdun?

A German repulse means a German tragedy. But if they succeed in their bold move on the center, and separate the allied armies, they will gain a very great strategic success and can then turn their attention to the investment of a segment of the fortifications of Paris.

Meanwhile the official *communiques* given out at three P.M. and at eleven P.M., at the Military Government of Paris, are, to say the least, hopeful. Every attempt to break through the French lines on the Ourcq has failed. No change noted on the center and on the allied right.

At two this afternoon I saw a small, low, dusty motor-car come spinning along the Boulevard des Invalides, containing four soldiers, who had with them two German flags, captured this morning during the fighting near the Ourcq. They were bringing their trophies to General Gallieni, who conferred the Military Medal--the highest French distinction for valor in action--on the reserve infantry soldier Guillemard, who captured one of these flags in a hand-to-hand encounter. The flag belonged to the Thirty-sixth Prussian Infantry Regiment, the Magdeburg Fusiliers, and had been decorated with the Iron Cross in 1870.

One of the French biplanes that scour the sky daily in search of German *taubes* met with sad disaster yesterday while flying over the Bois de Vincennes. The aeroplane contained a lieutenant and a corporal of the aviation corps. A violent gust of wind capsized it, and it fell to the ground, burying the occupants in a heap of debris. When extricated, both were dead. A few moments after the biplane struck the earth, either its motor, or the bombs that it had on board, exploded, and four passers-by were killed by flying fragments. Two of them were ten-year-old lads. A little girl and several other persons were more or less bruised. It so happened that I had watched this biplane from the Boulevard de Courcelles as it soared over Paris at a height of fifteen hundred meters. It was very steady in its movements and was going in an easterly direction. This must have been some ten minutes before the catastrophe.

The committee of the National Society of Fine Arts held a meeting today at the Grand Palais, to render aid to painters, sculptors, and artists in need of assistance, without regard to nationality, passed resolutions of indignation at the injury of works of art in France and Belgium committed by the German armies, and at the destruction of the objects of art solicited by Germany and entrusted by France to the International Exhibition at Leipsic, and unanimously voted to strike from the list of members the names of all artists of German nationality.

The art critic of the *Gil Blas*, M. Louis Vauxelles, whose scathing criticisms of the "classic" *pompier* academic school of painting and of sculpture, and whose intelligent censure of the extreme "futurist" clique elicit the hearty approval of all true lovers of art, in the United States, as well as in France, is serving as a simple soldier in an infantry regiment, but finds time occasionally to write to the *Intransigeant* picturesque descriptions of military life.

I received a letter from a friend at Tours, where the refugees are becoming less numerous, but the hospitals on the contrary are nearly full of wounded. Comtesse Paul de Pourtales is doing splendid work there as the head of the Red Cross, and M. Gaston Menier, the popular senator, a warm personal friend of Mr. Andrew Carnegie and the owner of the great chocolate works, has turned his Chateau of Chenonceaux into a perfectly organized hospital with a corps of surgeons and professional nurses, which he maintains at his own expense. Nearly a hundred French wounded are already being cared for in the Chenonceaux hospital. As soon as they get well enough, they are sent back to rejoin their regiments. All the villas in the neighborhood of Tours are already leased to families that have gone away from Paris.

In accordance with the notices of the Military Governor of Paris, I was vaccinated against smallpox to-day, together with all those now living in the house--in all twelve persons.

Mr. William G. Sharp, who has been appointed to succeed Mr. Myron T. Herrick as American Ambassador in France, remains here with his son, George, and is preparing to make himself familiar with the situation, so that when the proper time comes, he may take over his office. Mr. Sharp is already making headway with his somewhat theoretical knowledge of French. He told me that the war had upset many diplomatic and other precedents. "It is quite obvious," he said, "that at this critical period, Mr. Herrick could not desert his post, where his knowledge and experience have been so valuable." Mr. Sharp added: "It is needless to say that there will be no change of policy with my arrival as Ambassador to France. The friendship between the United States and France was never firmer than it is to-day. Personally, I am a fervent admirer of France, of French art, culture, and science.

"Probably no country in the world is more universally admired for its high degree of civilization than France. But it is my duty, as the future representative of the United States, to be absolutely neutral in everything concerning the present conflict. It cannot be too strongly stated that the United States Government will not swerve from its attitude of strict neutrality. The more impartial we remain, the stronger our position will be, and the better it will be, indeed, for all the belligerents when the time comes for discussing the conclusion of peace.

"For I shall not be indiscreet if I give voice to the thought held by many people that the role of the United States is bound to be a most important one at that moment.

"President Wilson's recent offer," he said, "was timely, and although every one knew that it could not then be accepted, yet it had the effect of setting men's minds thinking.

"What nation could be more fitted than the United States to take the lead in the peace negotiations?" asked Mr. Sharp. "In our nation are amalgamated all the races now at war. Our sincerity is undoubted. Our natural position of impartiality and neutrality is such that America's voice would be surely listened to at the opportune moment."

Mr. Sharp himself belongs to several peace organizations in America. He believes that after the present war there will be a complete revulsion of public opinion throughout the world in favor of peace. Never, he said, will there have been a riper moment for some scheme of general disarmament.

Mr. Sharp would like to see the United States a party to an epoch-making treaty sealing such an international accord. In this respect he believes that, atrocious as this European conflagration is, good will be the outcome for all nations, whoever the victors may be, if Europe reaps a lasting peace.

Mr. Sharp comes to Paris with a general knowledge of international political affairs, having served as a member in the United States Congress for three terms, and holding position of ranking member of the Foreign Affairs Committee at the time of his appointment.

Thursday, September 10.

Thirty-ninth day of the war. Cloudy weather, with a brisk shower and some thunder at three this afternoon. Afterwards fine. Southerly wind. Temperature at five P.M. 22 degrees centigrade.

Favorable news was communicated at eleven o'clock this evening at the headquarters at the Invalides. After four days of steady fighting, the allied left wing has crossed the Marne near Charly and driven back the enemy sixty kilometers, the British taking many prisoners and machine guns. Near Sezanne, the Prussian Guard Corps has been driven back, north of the marshes of St. Gond. No change is noted in relative positions on the allied center and right, where fighting still continues with great violence.

I went to the official press bureau at three this afternoon and met there M. Arthur Meyer, the genial and venerable editor of the ***Gaulois***, and about forty French and foreign journalists. M. Arthur Meyer, as "dean" of our calling, had a pleasant word and smile for all. Just before the official ***communique***, the director of the Press Bureau, Commandant Klotz, former Minister of Finance, instructed his assistant to notify all present that "any reproduction of or even allusion to the interview published in an American morning paper (the ***Paris Herald***) with an American diplomatist would not pass the censor if handed in at the telegraph or cable offices, and also that its appearance in any French newspaper was prohibited. The reason for this is that the interview might cause misunderstanding, and that it merely reflected the personal opinions of a private individual who in no way was an accredited representative of the United States."

This "official rebuke" was of course intended for Mr. William G. Sharp, whose interview was printed in today's ***Herald***. According to European custom, diplomacy is a special calling or profession like those of the soldier, sailor, lawyer, or physician. Amateur diplomacy has no place in Europe, and to the French mind, the presence in Paris of an unaccredited, although designated, ambassador, who expresses his personal opinions on every subject, while there is a duly accredited ambassador here, is an anomaly, causing no little annoyance to the authorities, and tending to hamper and discredit the official representative of the United States in Paris.

It is whispered that this "diplomatic indiscretion" of Mr. Sharp may lead to a refusal of the French Government, when the time comes, to grant his credentials. All the more so, because when Mr. Sharp was first spoken of as a possible ambassador to Russia, the Russian Foreign Office notified Washington that Mr. Sharp was not exactly a ***persona grata***, owing to certain public statements attributed to him concerning the attitude of the Russian Government in regard to passports to Jews of American and other nationalities. When Mr. Sharp was nominated as American Ambassador to France, the French Foreign Office discreetly inquired at St. Petersburg whether the Russian Government had any objection to Mr. Sharp being accepted in Paris as the United States Ambassador. The reply from St. Petersburg was that "there were no objections," consequently the usual intimation was given by the Quai d'Orsay that Mr. Sharp would be an agreeable person in Paris. The arrival here of Mr. Sharp, in the midst of the war, and his interview on the situation, however, has not influenced the French officials at the Foreign Office in his favor. Mr.

Sharp is unquestionably a patriotic, clear-headed, capable, and highly intelligent representative of our countrymen, and moreover, he is now obtaining diplomatic experience.

Spain has also had some tribulation with its ambassadors to France. When President Poincare and the French Cabinet decided to transfer the seat of government to Bordeaux, the Spanish Ambassador, Marquis de Villa Urrutia, was about to quit Paris with President Poincare, but the King of Spain wished his representative to remain in Paris. The marquis, however, to use an American expression, got "cold feet" and expressed a wish to go to Bordeaux. When this news reached King Alfonso, it so happened that Lieutenant-general de los Monteros, Marquis de Valtierra, Captain-general of Northern Spain at Burgos and San Sebastian, was in conference with the king. King Alfonso asked the Marquis de Valtierra where in his opinion would be the proper place in France for the Spanish Ambassador. "Why," was the quick reply, "Paris, of course." "Well," said the king, "that is not the opinion of the Marquis de Villa Urrutia, but it is also my own opinion, and I have now decided to send you to Paris as my ambassador!" Consequently, the Marquis de Villa Urrutia was forthwith replaced by the Marquis de Valtierra, who is already duly installed in the Spanish Embassy in the Boulevard de Courcelles. The new Spanish Ambassador speaks English perfectly, as well as French, and he is a personal friend of Ambassador Herrick.

The condition at the outbreak of the war of some of the French fortresses in the north near the Belgian frontier, as well as around Rheims and Vitry-le-Francois, for which the French Chamber of Deputies refused in 1899 to vote appropriations, is being paid for a thousandfold to-day. In 1885, when experiments made at Malmaison with the newly-invented torpedo shells, then about to be adopted by the German artillery, showed that no forts could resist them unless provided with armor plates and with *beton* protection for men and ammunition, a new plan of defence was drawn up. As the cost of the new armor and protection for the forts was very great, it was decided to *declasser* a number of fortresses, among which were Lille, Douai, Arras, Landrecies, Peronne, Vitry-le-Francois, and others. It had already been foreseen that the main German attack would some day be made through Luxemburg and Belgium. The fortresses of Maubeuge, Charlemont (Givet), Montmedy, and Longwy then became of supreme importance, for the defence of northern France against an invading army through Belgium. The Chamber of Deputies persistently refused to vote the necessary money, and the result of this want of foresight became painfully apparent during the present war, when the Germans made their broad sweep from Belgium to Compiegne, meeting on their way with no permanent works of defence.

The civil and religious wedding of Mr. James Gordon Bennett, proprietor of the ***New York Herald***, with Baroness George de Reuter took place to-day at the Town Hall of the ninth arrondissement of Paris, and at the American Episcopal Church of the Holy Trinity, in the Avenue de l'Alma. The witnesses of the bride were the Duc de Camastra and Vicomte de Breteuil. Those for Mr. Bennett were the American Ambassador, Mr. Herrick, and Professor Albert Robin, the well-known scientist and member of the French Academy of Medicine. The bride was the widow of Baron George de Reuter, and was formerly Miss Potter of Baltimore. The ceremonies were very simple, the only guests being Mrs. Herrick and the Vicomtesse de Breteuil. The ceremony in the church was performed by the Reverend Doctor Watson. Those present afterwards took tea at the residence of Mrs. Bennett in the Rue de Lubeck. The day before the wedding Mr. Bennett had been confirmed by the Reverend Doctor Watson in the faith of the American Episcopal Church. It will be remembered that Mr. Bennett's father was a Scotch Roman Catholic, while his mother was an Irish Protestant, a combination that seldom occurs, and which often induced Mr. Bennett to playfully remark: "I take after both my father and my mother, for when I find myself surrounded by genial conviviality, I feel that I am an Irishman, but when amidst grave cares and weighty business, I am a Scotchman."

Friday, September 11.

Fortieth day of the war. Overcast sky from dawn to noon, then steady, heavy rain all the afternoon. Southwest wind, blowing in gusts. Thermometer at five P.M. 17 degrees centigrade.

The Germans continue to retire north of the Marne towards Soissons. The British army has captured eleven guns, stores, ammunition, and fifteen hundred prisoners. The German retreat measures seventy kilometers in four days. All seems to go well with the allies. The heavy rain is bad for the German retreat, especially in the swampy ground they must pass through.

All this cheerful news from the front gives renewed confidence to the two millions of Parisians remaining at home, who begin to feel that there is no longer any imminent danger of being besieged.

What might be called a side-issue of the war appeared to-day in the shape of a new English daily newspaper published in Paris, called the ***Paris Daily Post***. It consists of a small single sheet--the ***Figaro***, and the ***Echo de Paris***, are the only papers now printed on double sheets--and in an editorial note declares that its policy is to "preach courage and confidence." It is an unpretentious, lively, amusing little production and may eventually have a brilliant career.

Many of the wounded now coming in to the hospitals are being treated for rheumatism contracted in the trenches during days and nights of exposure to the rain. A man of the East Lancashire Regiment, who had his left arm smashed by a shell, said that when his detachment were attacked at dawn in a village near Compiegne, "the terrified women and children rushed into the streets in their night gowns. Their houses were being smashed like pie-crust. It made us feel badly to see some of these poor women and children blown to pieces by the German shells. We tried to put them in whatever shelter was available."

Professor Pierre Delbet, of the Paris Faculty of Medicine, relates an extraordinary conversation between a young general commanding a division of the Prussian Guard Corps and Doctor Delbet's mother, who is a venerable lady of seventy-seven. Professor Delbet went yesterday to visit his mother at her country house situated in a village on the Grand Morin River, in the heart of the region where the fighting took place a few days ago. Madame Delbet's house is in the center of the village, and on her grounds a small wooden bridge connects the courtyard and flower garden with the vegetable garden on the other bank. There are two public bridges at the ends of the village, but these had been blown up by the French engineer soldiers. Last Friday morning the Germans arrived and smashed open the double gate of Madame Delbet's house. A young general, with an eyeglass fixed to his left eye, approached, while a soldier stood with a loaded revolver pointed at the old lady's head. The general remarked with politeness: "Madame, you will let us pass over your private bridge."

"I have no means of preventing you, but I warn you the bridge is not very solid."

"Ah! we will see to that."

The general gave orders, and in fifteen minutes the rickety bridge was braced up with three strong trusses. Then thirty soldiers were put on the bridge and jumped six times in unison at the word of command. After this test, the passage of troops began, while the ***pontoniers*** were repairing the two public bridges. The general approached Madame Delbet and with great courtesy placed two comfortable arm-chairs in a shady nook of the courtyard, and by an invitation that seemed to be a command, requested her to take a seat and see "the little Prussian review that would surely be interesting." The old lady sat beside the general and witnessed the ***defile*** that lasted seven hours--from 11.30 in the morning to 6.30 in the evening. The general scrutinized his men through his monocle. By and by he had his servant make some tea and toast, which he offered to his "hostess." While sipping tea, the general said: "Madame, when you become a German, as will surely be the case, you will be proud to recollect that you witnessed the passage of my troops over your bridge. I shall have a bronze tablet made and placed over your gate to commemorate the event."

When Madame Delbet protested, the general burst into a hearty laugh, and said: "Why, Madame, that is already settled. You cannot defend yourselves. Oh, yes! you have in mind your friends the English and your friends the Russians. But your good friends the English can only fight on the sea; they are of no value on land. As for the Russians, they don't know what an army is!"

At this moment the cavalry was passing over the bridge three abreast, and a lancer accidentally knocked over a bison's head that was hung in the court as a hunting trophy. The general severely reprimanded the trooper for his carelessness, and ordered the cavalry to cross two abreast. The conversation continued. Madame Delbet said that she thought the Russians had made considerable progress since the Japanese war. "Ah, yes, perhaps, but they have no real army ***yet!***"

The general then remarked: "Now about the French. You, yourself, Madame, must be aware, as you belong to a medical family, that the French are absolutely degenerate. The French have come to the end of their tether! I will let you into one of our secrets. This will be our ***ultimatum***, of which I have already read the text. Voila! We have decided to preserve a selection of the best and healthiest French-men and marry them to well-chosen North German girls of strong shape and build.

The result of this cross may be useful children. As to the other Frenchmen who survive the war, we have arranged to export them all to North and South America!"

"But, General," replied Madame Delbet, "we have had at least *some* success during the war."

"None whatever, Madame!"

"Why! We have captured some flags, anyway!"

"Where did you see that?"

"In the newspapers."

"The French, English, and American newspapers publish nothing but lies. In two days we shall be in Paris."

The general then gave a fresh turn to his eyeglass and called Madame Delbet's attention to the splendid physique, smart appearance, perfect order, method, and discipline of his troops. Madame Delbet admitted that this praise was fully justified, for the troops and horses were quite fresh, their uniforms and equipments were all spick and span, and the officers even wore fresh, unspotted gloves.

On Sunday the general took his departure. As he came to bid Madame Delbet good-by, he said: "I am going to Paris, Madame, and if I can be of any service to you there, kindly let me know." He then mounted his beautiful bay charger and rode away, followed by his staff. A couple of officers and a small detachment were left in the village.

Monday morning a German automobile dashed through the village at fourth speed. A sentry discharged his rifle as a signal. The same troops came trotting back again over the three bridges. One of them, who had been particularly attentive to Madame Delbet's maid, passed through the little courtyard. The maid slyly asked: "Is that the road to Paris?" She received the reply from her admirer: *"Plus Paris! Plus Paris!"*

Soon afterwards, some French dragoons galloped into the village over the bridges that the Germans had had no time to destroy. Then came two battalions of British infantry, at a double, over Madame Delbet's little garden bridge, and they deployed and opened fire on the retreating Germans. *"A Paris!"* and *"Plus Paris!"* are words that Madame Delbet says will always ring in her ears, for these phrases exactly describe the picturesque side glimpse of the war that passed in her pretty little courtyard, lined with rose-bushes, near her rustic wooden bridge. Professor Pierre Delbet vouches for the implicit accuracy of this characteristic conversation between his mother and the young lieutenant-general of the Prussian Guard Corps.

Saturday, September 12.

Forty-first day of the war. Rain and drizzle with southwesterly wind. Thermometer at five P.M. 15 degrees centigrade.

Good news. Six days' steady, hard fighting results in a French victory all along the line of the Marne. The German retreat is general. It is astonishing to see how quietly and calmly Parisians receive the welcome news. They are naturally delighted, but there are no wild outbursts of enthusiasm. They fully realize that this is merely one of the phases of the long, hard struggle.

Both General-in-Chief Joffre, and the German General Staff, foresaw that the great battle of the Marne must be decisive. General Joffre, in his order of the day of September 6, impressed upon his troops that "upon the coming battle the salvation of the country would depend," and admonished his soldiers that "if they should be unable to advance further, they must hold their ground or be killed on the spot, rather than retire." When the French cavalry made a sudden dash into Vitry-le-Francois and entered the house that had been occupied by the headquarters staff of the Eighth Army Corps, which had been hastily abandoned a few minutes before, they found, signed by Lieutenant-general Tulff von Tscheppe und Werdenbach, a general order which ran as follows:

Vitry-le-Francois, September 7, 10.30 A.M.--The goal pursued by our long and painful marches is reached. The principal French forces have had to accept battle after withdrawing continually. The great decision is undoubtedly near at hand. To-morrow, therefore, the total forces of the German army, as well as all those of our army corps, will have to be engaged all along the line going from Paris to Verdun. To save the happiness and honor of Germany, I expect from each officer and soldier, despite the hard and heroic fighting of the last few days, that he will accomplish his duty entirely and to his last breath. All depends upon the result of to-morrow's battle.

Sunday, September 13.

Forty-second day of the war. Cloudy weather, with strong westerly wind. Temperature at five P.M. 19 degrees centigrade.

I took one of the four daily trains for Havre, leaving the Gare Saint-Lazare, for my little country place in Vernon at 9.33 this morning and met in the same compartment Captain Decker, commander of the U.S.S. *Tennessee*, and two officers of his ship, which acts as a sort of ferry-boat for Americans stranded in France, carrying them to England. The *Tennessee* will sail from Havre to-morrow for Falmouth. The United States naval officers were in uniform and were constantly mistaken for British army officers. The military commanders at the stations came on board the train to ask if they could be of any service to them, and they were saluted with enthusiasm whenever they showed themselves. The train, conforming to the war regulations on all the railroads, went at the uniform prescribed pace of thirty miles an hour and stopped at every station, consequently we were four hours, instead of the usual one hour and ten minutes in getting to Vernon, which is only fifty miles from Paris. At Acheres, the junction with the northern lines, two carloads of wounded were hitched to our train. I found barricades on the outskirts of Vernon and the beautiful bridge, that had been blown up by the French in 1870 in a vain attempt to prevent the German occupation, was mined, so that it could be instantly destroyed. I found my little garden rather neglected, for the man who looks after it had been "mobilized" and is now lying in a hospital at Bordeaux, getting over a shrapnel wound in the leg. The place nevertheless was full of pears, peaches, figs, green corn, American squashes, beans, tomatoes, and no end of roses, gladioli, tobacco plant, hollyhocks, heliotrope, dahlias, morning-glories, verbena, and sunflowers.

I visited the Red Cross Hospital which, under the direction of Madame Steiner, wife of the mayor of Vernon, is doing splendid work at Vernonnet. There were two hundred wounded officers and soldiers here; among them were a dozen Belgians and a score of "Turcos," Algerian riflemen, who seemed very patient and docile. Some twenty wounded Germans here receive exactly the same treatment as the French. The German soldiers were from Prussian-Polish and Saxon regiments. The officers, five altogether, in a separate ward, were extremely reticent, and it was only with great difficulty that they could be induced to give their names and the numbers of their regiments. Happening to speak German, I acted as interpreter during the inspection by the French Medical Director. These young officers seemed greatly depressed and mortified at finding themselves prisoners.

While strolling about Vernon, I met Frederick MacMonnies, the American sculptor, and his wife, riding on bicycles. They had come from Giverny, some three miles away, where MacMonnies has his studio, not far from that of Claude Monet. MacMonnies told me that his studio was now a hospital with fifty beds, all of which were occupied by French and Belgians. Mrs. MacMonnies aids the surgeons in tending the wounded. During the approach of the Germans towards Beauvais, it was thought that Uhlans would soon appear at Vernon, and orders had been given to evacuate the hospitals. MacMonnies buried his valuable tapestries and rare works of French and Italian Renaissance art and prepared for the worst. Fortunately Vernon, Giverny, Paris, and its delightful neighborhood seems no longer to be in danger from invaders, and the people are recovering their peace of mind.

Monday, September 14.

Forty-third day of the war. Dull morning with slight showers. Sky overcast all the afternoon. Southwesterly wind blowing strong. Thermometer at five P.M. 16 degrees centigrade.

Back in Paris again, after a five hours' ride in a second-class compartment intended for ten, packed with twelve. Most of my fellow-passengers were refugees returning to Creil, Beaumont-sur-Oise, and other places north of Paris, now evacuated by the Germans.

Within living memory Paris has rarely seen so dense and vast a throng as that which assembled on Sunday in the Cathedral of Notre Dame for the special service of "intercession for the success of French arms," when Monseigneur Amette, Cardinal of Paris, preached a stirring sermon, exhorting people to "make extreme sacrifice for their native land." There must have been eight thousand persons in the cathedral. Not only were the five naves densely packed, but all the chapels along the side aisles were crowded with worshippers. An imposing procession was formed, including many religious bodies, associations of young girls, and all the Roman Catholic clergy of Paris. This cortege left the cathedral through the three gates of the great facade and took up its position between the basilica and the exterior railings. Here a temporary platform had been erected, from which Monseigneur Amette addressed the enormous crowd that filled the Rue d'Argonne, the Pont Notre Dame, and the Place Notre Dame, right up to the Prefecture of Police. After the Cardinal had pronounced the benediction, the crowd joined with impressive solemnity in the invocation of Sainte-Genevieve, Saint-Denis, Joan of Arc, and other saints on behalf of the French armies, and afterwards dispersed quietly and reverently.

Tuesday, September 15.

Forty-fourth day of the war. Gray, cloudy day, with occasional glimpses of sunshine. Brisk southwest wind. Temperature at five P.M. 15 degrees centigrade.

The Franco-British armies are close on the Germans' heels, but as everybody in Paris expected, the enemy is inclined to resist along their new lines. They are throwing up defences on the northwest, from the forest of l'Aigle to Craonne, and in the center from north of Rheims and the Camp of Chalons to Vienne-la-Ville on the west fringe of the Argonne.

The outlook seems so encouraging to the *Herald* that it has returned to antebellum conditions and reduced its price to fifteen centimes in France, and twenty-five centimes abroad, and usually appears in double sheet form.

Another American wedding to-day at the Town Hall of the sixth arrondissement. The bridegroom was Mr. John R. Clarke of New York, and the bride was Miss Marion Virginia Goode, also an American. Mr. Clarke went to the front immediately after the wedding, having volunteered in the British army for automobile service. He was arrayed in the regulation khaki uniform, and as he drove to the Mairie in his car just brought back from the Aisne with a number of bullet-holes in it, he was greeted with cheers. The bridal party was accompanied by Mr. Charles G. Loeb, of the American law firm of Valois, Loeb and Company.

The American Ambulance Hospital at Neuilly is doing really effective work. Among the wounded being treated there are French, Belgians, a few "Turcos," British officers and men, and some wounded German prisoners. Mrs. William K. Vanderbilt, who has been entrusted by the French Red Cross Association with the charge of the hospital, is indefatigable in her personal attention and efforts. The organization seems perfect. The funds so far subscribed exceed five hundred and seventy-four thousand francs. During a brief visit to the hospital, I noticed that

Mrs. Vanderbilt herself visited the wounded, and with the aid of her experienced staff of trained nurses, prepared them for surgical operations. Mrs. Vanderbilt wore the white Red Cross uniform. Half concealed about her neck was a double string of pearls. Rose-colored silk stockings were tipped with neat but serviceable white shoes, and in this attire she seemed to impersonate the presiding "good angel" of the hospital.

Through the courtesy of a friend who was going to Meaux in charge of a Red Cross automobile to distribute hospital stores to a field hospital near Plessis-Pacy, I had an opportunity to visit the scene of the recent battles along the Ourcq Canal, where General von Kluck's army met its first signal defeat. We came near to the villages of Chambry, Marcilly, Etrepilly, and Vincy--along the road from Meaux to Soissons--and found that the trenches dug by the Germans were filled with human corpses in thick, serried masses. Quicklime and straw had been thrown over them by the ton. Piles of bodies of men and of horses had been partially cremated in the most rudimentary fashion. The country seemed to be one endless charnel-house. The stench of the dead was appalling. Of the fifty odd houses that form the village of Etrepilly, not one remained intact. Some of them had been hit by a shell that penetrated through the roof, falling into the cellar, and by its explosion bringing down from garret or second story all the furniture in one confused mass of ruin. But many other houses had been simply sacked and looted. Cupboards, chests of drawers, and wardrobes were smashed open, and their contents scattered pell-mell in the streets, courtyards, and fields. Here was the portrait of an ancestor ripped to shreds by a bayonet; there was a child's cradle. An old-fashioned grandmother's armchair, with its cushions and ear-laps, lay smashed in fragments in the gutter. The village had fortunately been deserted by its inhabitants at the approach of the Germans, who, furious with rage, had looted, sacked, or wantonly destroyed whatever they found.

How thirsty the Germans were! The roads and fields and trenches were strewn with bottles, full or half-empty. The Germans must have been obliged to retreat suddenly, for heaps of unexploded shells for the three-inch and five-inch German field-guns were abandoned, and in wicker baskets were loads of three-inch unexploded shells, apparently about to be served to the gunners. Wanton, ruthless devastation everywhere! In a field was a wrecked aeroplane, a white and yellow *taube*, with its right wing reaching into the air, looking like some gigantic, wounded bird. Towards sunset, an automobile passed along the road through this terrible desolate valley of death. In it sat Monseigneur Marbeau, the venerable Bishop of Meaux--the successor of Bossuet, the famous "Eagle of Meaux"--who now and then raised his right finger aloft and then lowered it with the sign of the cross, as he pronounced benedictions on this vast charnel-house. A great number of German killed and wounded wearing uniforms of the Eleventh Prussian Infantry Regiment indicated that this corps had occupied the village of Etrepilly. As there were no civilian villagers noticed in this part of the country, this seems presumptive evidence that the Eleventh Prussian Infantry participated in this looting and wanton devastation.

As we were about to return to Paris, we met a friend of M. Gaston Menier on his way from the latter's country-house near Villa-Cotterets, where the memorable *chasses a courre* take place in the forest, which, under normal conditions, abounds in deer and stags. The chateau had been used as the headquarters of a brigade of Bavarian infantry. The house was intact, but some valuable furniture of the Louis XV period and some paintings had been destroyed, and the cellar, that had contained over two thousand bottles of excellent wine, including forty dozen bottles of champagne of the admirable vintage of 1904, had been "visited," and only seven bottles remained. The Bavarians, in pursuance of their practice in 1870, carried away all the clocks in the chateau.

Wednesday, September 16.

Forty-fifth day of the war. Sky heavily overcast. Southwesterly wind. Thermometer at five P.M. 15 degrees centigrade.

After the victorious contest of the Marne, we are now to have the gigantic struggle of the Aisne. The battle now engaged, because the Franco-British pursuit has compelled the German armies all along the line to reenforce their rear guards and fight, extends some one hundred and fifty miles in length on one front from Noyon, the heights north of Vic-sur-Aisne, Soissons, Rheims, to Ville-sur-Tourbe, west of the wooded ridge of the Argonne. Another "front," where vigorous defence is made by the German eastern armies, extends from the eastern border of the Argonne to the Forges forest north of Verdun, some fifty miles long.

Now that the Germans are fighting on the defensive, it is not too soon to record the fact that their extraordinary raid of a million of soldiers through Belgium to within twenty miles of Paris has failed. Nothing in military history approaches this avalanche of armies. The German invasion of France and the threat to invest and capture Paris is coming to an end. Yet this war can only be ended by an invasion either of France or of Germany being driven to a triumphant conclusion. The theater of war must soon be transferred from France to the east. The curtain falls upon the German invasion of France, and for the present, at least, Paris is no longer in danger. I see that a change has come over the Parisians, and I can read in their calm, confident faces the brighter phase that the war has assumed. Parisians of every class, from the **grande dame** of the Faubourg Saint-Germain to the **midinette** of the Rue de la Paix, or the professional beauty of Montmartre, are subdued and chastened by the sudden change that overtook their bright and exuberant existence. During this first period of the war, Paris assumed the aspect of a Scottish Sabbath. Feverish pursuit of pleasure, earnest hard work, luxury, elegant distinction, thrift, thronged boulevards, crowded theaters, clamorous music halls, frisky supper parties, tango teas, overflowing gaiety, sparkling wit, boisterous fun, and sly humor, have all vanished. The machinery of Parisian life is working at quarter speed. Streets are nearly deserted, except for rapidly flitting automobiles, used mostly for military purposes. The Rue de la Paix is a vacant pathway, where one might play lawn tennis all day long. Probably three fourths of the Paris shops are still closed. The underground trains are as yet few and far between. Now and then a tramway rumbles along the streets, but there is not a solitary omnibus running in the city. The popularity of the bicycle is regained, for well-to-do folk whose motor-cars have been requisitioned now make use of the humble wheel. The quaint, one-horse cab, evoking souvenirs of Muerger, Paul de Kock, and Guy de Maupassant, with venerable **cocher**, re-appears. There are some auto-taxicabs about, and their slowly increasing number indicates that Paris is beginning to shake off the paralysis imposed by the outbreak of the war. Undisturbed by the turmoil, the forty "immortal" Academicians are continuing their labors on the Dictionary of the Academy. They are approaching the end of the letter "E" and are to-day discussing, with singular actuality, the word "Exodus." May that mean the German exodus from French soil!

The Codes Of Hammurabi And Moses
W. W. Davies

QTY

The discovery of the Hammurabi Code is one of the greatest achievements of archaeology, and is of paramount interest, not only to the student of the Bible, but also to all those interested in ancient history...

Religion   **ISBN:** *1-59462-338-4*   **Pages:132**
MSRP $12.95

The Theory of Moral Sentiments
Adam Smith

QTY

This work from 1749. contains original theories of conscience amd moral judgment and it is the foundation for systemof morals.

Philosophy **ISBN:** *1-59462-777-0*   **Pages:536**
MSRP $19.95

Jessica's First Prayer
Hesba Stretton

QTY

In a screened and secluded corner of one of the many railway-bridges which span the streets of London there could be seen a few years ago, from five o'clock every morning until half past eight, a tidily set-out coffee-stall, consisting of a trestle and board, upon which stood two large tin cans, with a small fire of charcoal burning under each so as to keep the coffee boiling during the early hours of the morning when the work-people were thronging into the city on their way to their daily toil...

Childrens   **ISBN:** *1-59462-373-2*   **Pages:84**
MSRP $9.95

My Life and Work
Henry Ford

QTY

Henry Ford revolutionized the world with his implementation of mass production for the Model T automobile. Gain valuable business insight into his life and work with his own auto-biography... "We have only started on our development of our country we have not as yet, with all our talk of wonderful progress, done more than scratch the surface. The progress has been wonderful enough but..."

Biographies/   **ISBN:** *1-59462-198-5*   **Pages:300**
MSRP $21.95

The Art of Cross-Examination
Francis Wellman

QTY

I presume it is the experience of every author, after his first book is published upon an important subject, to be almost overwhelmed with a wealth of ideas and illustrations which could readily have been included in his book, and which to his own mind, at least, seem to make a second edition inevitable. Such certainly was the case with me; and when the first edition had reached its sixth impression in five months, I rejoiced to learn that it seemed to my publishers that the book had met with a sufficiently favorable reception to justify a second and considerably enlarged edition. ..

Reference   ISBN: *1-59462-647-2*

Pages:412

MSRP $19.95

On the Duty of Civil Disobedience
Henry David Thoreau

QTY

Thoreau wrote his famous essay, On the Duty of Civil Disobedience, as a protest against an unjust but popular war and the immoral but popular institution of slave-owning. He did more than write—he declined to pay his taxes, and was hauled off to gaol in consequence. Who can say how much this refusal of his hastened the end of the war and of slavery ?

Law   ISBN: *1-59462-747-9*

Pages:48

MSRP $7.45

Dream Psychology Psychoanalysis for Beginners
Sigmund Freud

QTY

Sigmund Freud, born Sigismund Schlomo Freud (May 6, 1856 - September 23, 1939), was a Jewish-Austrian neurologist and psychiatrist who co-founded the psychoanalytic school of psychology. Freud is best known for his theories of the unconscious mind, especially involving the mechanism of repression; his redefinition of sexual desire as mobile and directed towards a wide variety of objects; and his therapeutic techniques, especially his understanding of transference in the therapeutic relationship and the presumed value of dreams as sources of insight into unconscious desires.

Psychology   ISBN: *1-59462-905-6*

Pages:196

MSRP $15.45

The Miracle of Right Thought
Orison Swett Marden

QTY

Believe with all of your heart that you will do what you were made to do. When the mind has once formed the habit of holding cheerful, happy, prosperous pictures, it will not be easy to form the opposite habit. It does not matter how improbable or how far away this realization may see, or how dark the prospects may be, if we visualize them as best we can, as vividly as possible, hold tenaciously to them and vigorously struggle to attain them, they will gradually become actualized, realized in the life. But a desire, a longing without endeavor, a yearning abandoned or held indifferently will vanish without realization.

Self Help   ISBN: *1-59462-644-8*

Pages:360

MSRP $25.45

QTY

The Rosicrucian Cosmo-Conception Mystic Christianity *by Max Heindel*   ISBN: *1-59462-188-8*   **$38.95**
The Rosicrucian Cosmo-conception is not dogmatic, neither does it appeal to any other authority than the reason of the student. It is: not controversial, but is: sent forth in the, hope that it may help to clear...   *New Age/Religion Pages 646*

Abandonment To Divine Providence *by Jean-Pierre de Caussade*   ISBN: *1-59462-228-0*   **$25.95**
"The Rev. Jean Pierre de Caussade was one of the most remarkable spiritual writers of the Society of Jesus in France in the 18th Century. His death took place at Toulouse in 1751. His works have gone through many editions and have been republished...   *Inspirational/Religion Pages 400*

Mental Chemistry *by Charles Haanel*   ISBN: *1-59462-192-6*   **$23.95**
Mental Chemistry allows the change of material conditions by combining and appropriately utilizing the power of the mind. Much like applied chemistry creates something new and unique out of careful combinations of chemicals the mastery of mental chemistry...   *New Age Pages 354*

The Letters of Robert Browning and Elizabeth Barret Barrett 1845-1846 vol II   ISBN: *1-59462-193-4*   **$35.95**
by Robert Browning and Elizabeth Barrett   *Biographies Pages 596*

Gleanings In Genesis (volume I) *by Arthur W. Pink*   ISBN: *1-59462-130-6*   **$27.45**
Appropriately has Genesis been termed "the seed plot of the Bible" for in it we have, in germ form, almost all of the great doctrines which are afterwards fully developed in the books of Scripture which follow...   *Religion/Inspirational Pages 420*

The Master Key *by L. W. de Laurence*   ISBN: *1-59462-001-6*   **$30.95**
In no branch of human knowledge has there been a more lively increase of the spirit of research during the past few years than in the study of Psychology, Concentration and Mental Discipline. The requests for authentic lessons in Thought Control, Mental Discipline and...   *New Age/Business Pages 422*

The Lesser Key Of Solomon Goetia *by L. W. de Laurence*   ISBN: *1-59462-092-X*   **$9.95**
This translation of the first book of the "Lernegton" which is now for the first time made accessible to students of Talismanic Magic was done, after careful collation and edition, from numerous Ancient Manuscripts in Hebrew, Latin, and French...   *New Age/Occult Pages 92*

Rubaiyat Of Omar Khayyam *by Edward Fitzgerald*   ISBN:*1-59462-332-5*   **$13.95**
Edward Fitzgerald, whom the world has already learned, in spite of his own efforts to remain within the shadow of anonymity, to look upon as one of the rarest poets of the century, was born at Bredfield, in Suffolk, on the 31st of March, 1809. He was the third son of John Purcell...   *Music Pages 172*

Ancient Law *by Henry Maine*   ISBN: *1-59462-128-4*   **$29.95**
The chief object of the following pages is to indicate some of the earliest ideas of mankind, as they are reflected in Ancient Law, and to point out the relation of those ideas to modern thought.   *Religiom/History Pages 452*

Far-Away Stories *by William J. Locke*   ISBN: *1-59462-129-2*   **$19.45**
"Good wine needs no bush, but a collection of mixed vintages does. And this book is just such a collection. Some of the stories I do not want to remain buried for ever in the museum files of dead magazine-numbers an author's not unpardonable vanity..."   *Fiction Pages 272*

Life of David Crockett *by David Crockett*   ISBN: *1-59462-250-7*   **$27.45**
"Colonel David Crockett was one of the most remarkable men of the times in which he lived. Born in humble life, but gifted with a strong will, an indomitable courage, and unremitting perseverance...   *Biographies/New Age Pages 424*

Lip-Reading *by Edward Nitchie*   ISBN: *1-59462-206-X*   **$25.95**
Edward B. Nitchie, founder of the New York School for the Hard of Hearing, now the Nitchie School of Lip-Reading, Inc, wrote "LIP-READING Principles and Practice". The development and perfecting of this meritorious work on lip-reading was an undertaking...   *How-to Pages 400*

A Handbook of Suggestive Therapeutics, Applied Hypnotism, Psychic Science   ISBN: *1-59462-214-0*   **$24.95**
by Henry Munro   *Health/New Age/Health/Self-help Pages 376*

A Doll's House: and Two Other Plays *by Henrik Ibsen*   ISBN: *1-59462-112-8*   **$19.95**
Henrik Ibsen created this classic when in revolutionary 1848 Rome. Introducing some striking concepts in playwriting for the realist genre, this play has been studied the world over.   *Fiction/Classics/Plays 308*

The Light of Asia *by sir Edwin Arnold*   ISBN: *1-59462-204-3*   **$13.95**
In this poetic masterpiece, Edwin Arnold describes the life and teachings of Buddha. The man who was to become known as Buddha to the world was born as Prince Gautama of India but he rejected the worldly riches and abandoned the reigns of power when...   *Religion/History/Biographies Pages 170*

The Complete Works of Guy de Maupassant *by Guy de Maupassant*   ISBN: *1-59462-157-8*   **$16.95**
"For days and days, nights and nights, I had dreamed of that first kiss which was to consecrate our engagement, and I knew not on what spot I should put my lips..."   *Fiction/Classics Pages 240*

The Art of Cross-Examination *by Francis L. Wellman*   ISBN: *1-59462-309-5*   **$26.95**
Written by a renowned trial lawyer, Wellman imparts his experience and uses case studies to explain how to use psychology to extract desired information through questioning.   *How-to/Science/Reference Pages 408*

Answered or Unanswered? *by Louisa Vaughan*   ISBN: *1-59462-248-5*   **$10.95**
Miracles of Faith in China   *Religion Pages 112*

The Edinburgh Lectures on Mental Science (1909) *by Thomas*   ISBN: *1-59462-008-3*   **$11.95**
This book contains the substance of a course of lectures recently given by the writer in the Queen Street Hall, Edinburgh. Its purpose is to indicate the Natural Principles governing the relation between Mental Action and Material Conditions...   *New Age/Psychology Pages 148*

Ayesha *by H. Rider Haggard*   ISBN: *1-59462-301-5*   **$24.95**
Verily and indeed it is the unexpected that happens! Probably if there was one person upon the earth from whom the Editor of this, and of a certain previous history, did not expect to hear again.   *Classics Pages 380*

Ayala's Angel *by Anthony Trollope*   ISBN: *1-59462-352-X*   **$29.95**
The two girls were both pretty, but Lucy who was twenty-one who supposed to be simple and comparatively unattractive, whereas Ayala was credited, as her Bombwhat romantic name might show, with poetic charm and a taste for romance. Ayala when her father died was nineteen...   *Fiction Pages 484*

The American Commonwealth *by James Bryce*   ISBN: *1-59462-286-8*   **$34.45**
An interpretation of American democratic political theory. It examines political mechanics and society from the perspective of Scotsman James Bryce   *Politics Pages 572*

Stories of the Pilgrims *by Margaret P. Pumphrey*   ISBN: *1-59462-116-0*   **$17.95**
This book explores pilgrims religious oppression in England as well as their escape to Holland and eventual crossing to America on the Mayflower, and their early days in New England...   *History Pages 268*

QTY

The Fasting Cure *by Sinclair Upton*　　　　　　　　　　　　　ISBN: *1-59462-222-1*　**$13.95**
*In the Cosmopolitan Magazine for May, 1910, and in the Contemporary Review (London) for April, 1910, I published an article dealing with my experi-
ences in fasting. I have written a great many magazine articles, but never one which attracted so much attention... New Age/Self Help/Health Pages 164*

Hebrew Astrology *by Sepharial*　　　　　　　　　　　　　　　ISBN: *1-59462-308-2*　**$13.45**
*In these days of advanced thinking it is a matter of common observation that we have left many of the old landmarks behind and that we are now pressing
forward to greater heights and to a wider horizon than that which represented the mind-content of our progenitors...　Astrology Pages 144*

Thought Vibration or The Law of Attraction in the Thought World　　ISBN: *1-59462-127-6*　**$12.95**

by William Walker Atkinson　　　　　　　　　　　　　　　　*Psychology/Religion Pages 144*

Optimism *by Helen Keller*　　　　　　　　　　　　　　　　ISBN: *1-59462-108-X*　**$15.95**
*Helen Keller was blind, deaf, and mute since 19 months old, yet famously learned how to overcome these handicaps, communicate with the world, and
spread her lectures promoting optimism. An inspiring read for everyone...　Biographies/Inspirational Pages 84*

Sara Crewe *by Frances Burnett*　　　　　　　　　　　　　　ISBN: *1-59462-360-0*　**$9.45**
*In the first place, Miss Minchin lived in London. Her home was a large, dull, tall one, in a large, dull square, where all the houses were alike, and all the
sparrows were alike, and where all the door-knockers made the same heavy sound...　Childrens/Classic Pages 88*

The Autobiography of Benjamin Franklin *by Benjamin Franklin*　　ISBN: *1-59462-135-7*　**$24.95**
*The Autobiography of Benjamin Franklin has probably been more extensively read than any other American historical work, and no other book of its kind
has had such ups and downs of fortune. Franklin lived for many years in England, where he was agent...　Biographies/History Pages 332*

Name	
Email	
Telephone	
Address	
City, State ZIP	

☐ **Credit Card**　　　　　☐ **Check / Money Order**

Credit Card Number	
Expiration Date	
Signature	

*Please Mail to:　Book Jungle
　　　　　　　　PO Box 2226
　　　　　　　　Champaign, IL 61825
or Fax to:　　　630-214-0564*

ORDERING INFORMATION

web: *www.bookjungle.com*
email: *sales@bookjungle.com*
fax: *630-214-0564*
mail: *Book Jungle PO Box 2226 Champaign, IL 61825*
or PayPal *to sales@bookjungle.com*

Please contact us for bulk discounts

DIRECT-ORDER TERMS

**20% Discount if You Order
Two or More Books**
Free Domestic Shipping!
Accepted: Master Card, Visa,
Discover, American Express